Karen —

I love you my friend! I trust you will enjoy this book about a passion we both share.

Ken Hayes

BROKEN TRUST

CHILDREN IN PERIL

KENNEY
OLDHAM HAYES

ISBN 978-1-66789-713-4 (Print)

ISBN 978-1-66789-714-1 (eBook)

DEDICATION

THIS BOOK IS DEDICATED TO ALL UNWANTED, FOR-gotten, abandoned, and abused kids in the foster care system. Many of the children were ripped in the middle of the night from their sleep with only the clothes on their backs. Many of these children lay awake at night wondering where their mommy and daddy might be. Wondering why they are not 'good enough' to be loved. Always curious about why parents fight and throw punches at them in anger, or a parent completely disappears from their life.

All the children in the streets are just looking for someone to care for them, just love them, and just be a part of a forever family. All those children who believed one lie after the other by their parents that they would be back, only to circle again and again in the foster care system.

More specifically this dedication to those children who trust enough to be in a foster care home, trying to make the best of it even if they are sexually abused and too ashamed to speak not knowing who to trust. To those children who have no one consistent in their life because a new social worker is assigned regularly.

Don't get me wrong, the foster care system when it works is fabulous. There are just too many children coming into the system at an alarming rate, for the number of dedicated foster parents available to these children. Along with a falling number of people going into Social Services, and never enough funds to hire if they could find qualified individuals.

This book is dedicated to them. They are the ones paying the penalty for adults, politicians, and their own government failing miserably to care so little about the children, and fixing a 40-year-old broken system, that is always very short of money, leadership, services, and attention to this underdeveloped, underfunded, most critical cause.

God bless each child who suffers at the hands of trusting adults. May one day we get enough attention for you that you don't have to stay in a system for years only to be released at 18 for find a way for yourself with no skill set. May God hold you closer every time you are sexually harmed, trafficked, are you are forced to sleep in the streets, or put in slavery in another country. May God give you strength, courage, and humility to stand up and faces the demons, knowing one day there will be an answer for the horror you have been through.

Trust: The foundation of relationships which gives confidence in something or believing in someone because you feel safe.

INTRODUCTION

MAGINE BEING FOUR-YEARS-OLD AND RIPPED FROM the only home and parents you know, whisked away in the middle of the night with only the clothes on your back, then placed in a home with complete strangers. Now, imagine that being one of your own children.

According to the National Foster Care Facts and Statistics, Child Welfare Information Gateway, there are over 400,000 children in foster care, a number growing at a rapid rate primarily because of mental illness and especially drugs. The average child waiting to be adopted from the U.S. Foster Care system is eight years old, but many of them are newborns and infants.

The children will face a great deal of pain, anxiety, and panic in their inability to understand the situation they are in. In many cases they will never find their "forever" home.

The nightmare stories these children live through are true, both before and often after they enter the Foster Care System. The systems are broken. The laws are seldom in the children's best interest, no

1

matter how much the courts and the lawmakers may pretend they are. It has been well over forty years since there have been significant changes to the system.

Their advocates within the Foster Care System fight as hard as they can on the children's behalf. As you hear their stories throughout this book, the advocates will become your heroes. But they have to improvise and make plans up along the way that may or may not support the interest of the child. With an overcrowded court system, they are sometimes forced by the laws to look the other way when all children need is help to survive. There needs to be attention from our government. At the very least, real reform needs to make it onto the legislative agenda to prevent the type of stories that fill this book and the loves of the children caught in this terrible trap.

CHAPTER 1

THE WOMAN'S BODY WAS DRAPED OVER THE STEERING wheel with her head resting against the driver's window. She lay unconscious as a stream of blood flowed from cuts on her face and from her ears. Her right eye was almost swollen shut. The car in which she lay sat on the side of the road, its engine still running and the heater still trying to warm the inside of the car, even though outside the temperature was below freezing and the front passenger side door was open to the elements.

Blood-curdling screams poured from the back seat. A six-month-old baby girl, still strapped into her infant car seat, tossed her arms and legs in terror. The girl had pooped so much that it ran all over her car seat. Her face was a mask of fear and helplessness as her innocent little mind tried to bring reason to something she could not understand. She was too young to understand her situation or the feelings of total abandonment and bitter cold.

It was two in the morning when a large SUV pulled up behind the old beater car to see if everyone was okay. Harvey Waggoner, a 45-year-old highly paid corporate attorney, was headed home after a long trip of interviewing witnesses for an upcoming trial. It had been a very long day, and he was very tired from the flight from Chicago. He was really looking forward to getting to his new home here on the outskirts of Seattle. He had been staying at extended stay motels since arriving in Seattle. It took longer for him to find a place to buy than he expected. He was elated he had found a home outside of the main hubbub of Seattle. He had never been happier.

As he pulled up, he saw the car over at the side of the road with its engine running and the door open. Where the car was located was not a highly traveled road, rather a back road used mainly by people who lived out in this wilderness. Here in Washington State, on the Peninsula as it was called with its tall trees and dense forests and wildlife, darkness surrounded everything. It could be scary enough for anyone driving alone on the road, let alone stopped on the roadside. Harvey's gut knew something was desperately wrong.

He pulled in behind the parked car, not knowing what he was getting into or what he might find, but knowing what he was seeing wasn't normal. His heart was pounding out of his chest. He knew. He hesitated at first to get involved, but he knew he could not just drive away without checking first. He stopped and turned down the blaring radio in his own car that he was using to keep awake. He turned off his engine and carefully opened his door. Immediately, he heard the hair-raising screams of an infant. He rushed towards the noise from the passenger side of the car but stopped when he saw what looked like a person's body hanging over the steering wheel. He began shouting from the back of the car, "Hello, hello, do you need help?"

With his heart racing as though he'd been running for miles, he reached for the back door where he could see the baby strapped in a car seat. This door was locked so he cautiously bent down and looked through the open door in the front, peering in at woman with long hair and torn clothes who was bleeding and either dead or unconscious. Nevertheless, he called out to her, "Miss, Miss, Miss, are you alright?"

Since there was no response, he ran back to his own car and got his cell phone, dialing 911 as he returned to the car. He continued to call to the woman lodged in the driver's seat, "Miss, Miss, are you alright? I've called 911. Don't worry; they'll be here in a minute."

He reached his arm in from the front seat and unlocked the back door. The child seemed even more alarmed seeing this stranger and began wailing even louder to the point of having a hard time catching her breath. Harvey was not one for babies. He had never had children and didn't know what to do. He hoped good, old common sense would kick in. He unbuckled the baby's strap and reached in to pick the screaming child up. As he did so, he realized this baby was wet, dirty, and very smelly. He grabbed a blanket lying in the back seat and wrapped the infant up, holding her close and talking as calmly as he could.

In the distance, he heard the sirens of the police and, hopefully, the ambulance coming his way. In Harvey's mind they could not get there fast enough. He frantically but gently rocked the baby, hoping he could comfort the child enough to slow down its gasping between cries.

Harvey suddenly remembered that there was another person in this car, so he bent down to call out to the driver again. "Miss, Miss, can you hear me?" But there was no sign of movement, only the blood dripping down her hands onto the floor. He didn't know what else to do so he inspected the car as he waited for the rescue team's arrival. It didn't appear that the car had been in an accident. It was old and dilapidated, but it was parked off the road, the keys still in the ignition, and the radio blaring into the night. Harvey reached in and turned off the radio noise. "There," he thought, "that's better."

Harvey looked again into the back seat and spotted the diaper bag next to the seat. He reached into the bag to see if there was anything he could give the child to calm it, when he saw her name tag on the bag: Anna Taylor.

"Anna," he said softly. "Anna. It's going to be okay. You're safe, Anna." He continued calling her by name, and she began to relax enough to stop screaming, although she continued to cry in her tiny, hoarse voice.

At last, two police cars arrived along with an ambulance and EMTs. The officers leapt out of their cars with weapons pointed at him as one policeman instructed Harvey not to move. Harvey didn't move except to continue rocking the child. He told the police, "This is how I found the car. The child was strapped into her car seat and I took her out because she's been screaming since I got here. I called out several times to the woman, but she never answered. Honestly, she doesn't even look like she's alive."

The policemen relaxed a little and went to inspect the car. One EMT came over to Harvey while the other went to check on the driver. As the medic examined the baby, she resumed her screaming and crying. Finally, they told Harvey that the baby seemed physically okay, then he left to help the other EMT and the officers.

One of the policemen who seemed to be in charge walked over to Harvey and gently pulled the blanket from Anna's face. She immediately screamed out in terror again. The officer jumped back as

Harvey began comforting her again. Certain that whatever this baby had gone through must have been unbelievable trauma for such a young infant. Harvey was scared for Anna now because he had no idea if this child's mother was dead or alive. Tears began streaming down Harvey's cheek as he looked down at the tiny girl he was holding who looked at him as if to say, "Help me please!" Harvey shuddered at the thought of what might lie ahead for her.

For a few moments, Harvey stood so lost in his thoughts, that he had to shake his head to get back to reality when he heard one of the policemen on the other side of the car say, "Yep, this is her. This is the lady that was at the station looking for help several hours ago."

CHAPTER 2

A HALF-HOUR PASSED BY WITH ANNA SETTLED IN Harvey's arms. the policeman came over to Harvey to suggest he sit inside the car for warmth until CPS arrived. Meanwhile, the EMTs worked on the woman in the car. She was in bad shape.

After leaving him standing there all this time, one of the policemen finally approached Harvey and introduced himself as Officer Pete Murdock. "Would you mind staying here for a while and holding this baby?" the officer continued. "It seems you've got her calmed down a little. Maybe the two of you can sit in your car for warmth. I'm going to need to ask you a few questions either here or at the station, depending on what the Chief says."

Harvey agreed to stay and made his way over to his passenger side. He eased down into the seat with Anna sleeping lightly in his arms. She had calmed down a lot although Harvey could still feel her little body jerking in her sleep.

Meanwhile, Officer Murdock took a step back and pulled his cell phone out of his pocket, calling his boss, Sheriff Bloom of Kitsap

County. Pete assumed that the Chief, as he called his boss, was at the station because he had been working on some unknown project and had developed a pattern of staying till the wee hours of the morning and coming in late on morning shifts.

The officer knew this was an unusual case, especially for this small county, and also that a child was involved, which meant involvement with outside agencies. The Chief was never happy about "outside agencies" nosing around his cases. Nevertheless, this case could put them on the map. *A wife beating and an infant let out in the cold and alone is something the Chief would want to know about,* Pete thought. Although Sheriff Bloom had been Pete's good friend for a long while, Pete didn't dare cross him. Bloom required all the on-duty patrol officers to be ready to "walk the plank" if somebody didn't follow the rules.

Sheriff Walter Bloom had a degree in criminal law from the University of Southern California and had come to Port Orchards after being in law enforcement for 18 years in California. He replaced the current "loved by the citizens" sheriff on his retirement. Bloom had vast experience and knowledge, although of course he saw things differently from the homegrown officers in Kitsap County. Over time Bloom had made a mark by putting petty criminals behind bars, making the whole community feel safer. Of course, there weren't very many "big criminals" coming to Port Orchard to operate. Pete went out of his way to learn as much as possible from him when he joined the department five years earlier, so the two formed a strong bond.

Pete knew Sheriff Bloom and his wife of 30 years had separated and was headed for divorce. They were under a lot of pressure since Walter Bloom was an icon in Port Orchard. Pete wondered if the marriage problems were also a factor in the Chief's odd, late hours at the station.

"No, don't bring them to the station," insisted Sheriff Bloom. "I don't want to upset that child any more than possible and I'd like CPS to see the environment we found her in. You can send the other guys back to the station but Pete, you stay with the guy. Don't let him mess with the crime scene or let him out of your sight. I'll send a team out to search and fingerprint the car. When they arrive, you can release the scene to them. We'll catch up when you get back here after the child gets picked up."

Pete was glad he called him, relieved to have the Chief take responsibility for the next steps. He put away his phone and headed back to where Harvey and the baby were sitting in his car.

"We're assuming that's the child's mother," he told Harvey as he explained about the wait. "She appears to have been beaten up pretty badly, but she's alive. We're taking her along to the hospital now." Both men watched as the EMTs carefully lifted the woman onto a stretcher and rolled her towards the ambulance.

After a while, Officer Pete went on. "CPS is a way out, so you can leave the child with me. But maybe we should try and clean her up a little. She stinks. Making a face, Pete began rummaging through her diaper bag and pulling out a clean diaper grinning as if he had discovered gold. "Here try this. And here are some baby wipes."

Harvey grunted and took Anna to the back of the SUV where they would have room for their maneuvers. Ever so gently, he laid Anna down, keeping her covered with the soiled blanket. She moaned in little gasps of breath when he put her on her back, but she remained asleep. Pete leaned up against the car like he was on a break and handed Harvey the diaper while opening the pack of wipes. He seemed more than relieved to do his police job instead of Harvey's task of cleaning this child.

Being an obsessive planner, Harvey always carried an extra jacket and blankets with a variety of items he might need in his car during the winter months. You never know when you might get stuck. There was also an earthquake preparedness bag, a couple of extra towels, and an old pair of sneakers and golf balls rolling around in the back. Prepared for everything.

Harvey built a wall around the baby using towels and jackets so she would not get too cold in the whipping wind, then he worked her little pants off her soaking. legs He negotiated each leg out of the stinky pants with surgical precision.

"See if there's an extra pair of pants in the bag," he instructed Pete as he wiped down her legs and bottom with wads of baby-wipes. So far so good, but he held up the diaper as if it were a jigsaw puzzle.

Officer Pete, seeing that Harvey was stumped, said, "Here, let me show you how that works." He opened the diaper and showed Harvey how to tell front from back and where the sticky things held it together. "I've had a couple of babies in my life before," the policeman explained.

Between the two, they were able to get Anna cleaned up and into the spare pants that Pete had found in the bag. Harvey took away the ruined blanket from the care and replaced it with his own, wrapping her tightly to keep her warm.

As Harvey picked her up, Anna opened her eyes. Once again, fear and trembling overcame the beautiful baby girl. She tried to cry, but it seemed as if her voice was gone. She had probably been screaming and crying for long before Harvey pulled up and found them. It seemed the little thing had cried her voice out.

Harvey held her close, calling her name and humming "Cat's in the cradle and the silver spoon, little boy blue and the man in the moon…" How odd that song had popped into his head. He had not heard it in years. But Anna stopped trembling and looked up at her new friend, even giving him a shy, little smile. Harvey's heart flipped a few times. He had read about hearts that melted like butter in a hot iron skillet but had never believed it until that moment. He smiled back, murmuring her name holding her close.

Harvey was amazed at how he was feeling about this little girl. He never had kids. He had wanted them, but his late wife Cassie did not. The two of them fought over that issue more than they did about money, sex, or anything else. He felt guilty about it in the end. Theirs had been a whirlwind romance, and the idea of children that never came up until after the marriage. Now, with Cassie gone, he was relieved and even glad they never had kids.

But he could feel how engaged he was with the tiny life that he was holding in his arms. All at once, it was desperately important to him what would happen next with Anna. Harvey was a good lawyer and knew a lot about the law in general, but he knew next to nothing about juvenile law. He worried how she would be handled and where she would go. It was going to be awful to wake her up and hand her to another stranger now that she had finally calmed down. He wasn't sure he could let her go. She looked so helpless and vulnerable all by herself. He worried that this little girl would not be able to handle one more trauma.

Harvey sat in the back of his car with Anna, waiting for CPS to arrive. Pete had released the other police car on the orders of his

Chief. If he had known that CPS would be so long, he would have taken Harvey and the child back to the station as well. *Too late to worry about that now*, he thought, as he and Harvey talked and waited.

Harvey had been up since four AM the morning before, Chicago time, and had been through countless hours interviewing witnesses in Chicago. He could feel his body responding to all of this drama that he had just been through. He learned about Pete's family and how much he loved his job and living on the Peninsula. Harvey explained that he had a small place on the water near Port Orchard and loved every minute he was there. Although he hated the long commute to downtown Seattle on Interstate 5 as well as the long ferry ride, since he only went to his office now and then, he could deal with the driving and traffic to live in such a pristine place. Thank goodness for technology, they agreed.

"So, you're a corporate lawyer, and you do what exactly?" asked Pete.

"Well, my role is to protect my client, of course, which is usually a big organization, usually valued over $500 million in assets. We make sure they get to keep their money and reputation," said Harvey. "Sorry to say, I'm not always on the side of justice because mostly it's a game of who can last the longest paying expensive attorney invoices," Harvey chuckled. "I mean, we follow the law, but like most things, everything is judged on interpretation and perception."

"So, are you the good guy or the bad one?" Pete asked.

Harvey laughed out loud, causing Anna to stir a little. He hushed his voice to answer, "I think that's a very good question, Pete, and one we'll leave for another time."

Harvey liked Pete. He seemed honest and very personable, a straight shooter. He thought he might look the policeman up at another time so they could get together for coffee or something. He did not have a lot of friends out on the peninsula.

The conversation ended abruptly as another car came towards them. They both hoped it was the CPS people at last. It was cold and creepy out there in the dark, even with the police around.

CHAPTER 3

AS THEY SAW THE LIGHTS PULLING UP VERY SLOWLY behind them, Officer Pete instinctively upholstered his weapon and got out of the car, telling Harvey to stay where he was. He moved closer to the bushes on the side of the road as if he expected an unwelcome visitor. Although Harvey had not known Pete for very long, he sensed a heightened urgency from his new friend. *Was Pete just being cautious or was there some real danger that he was unaware of,* Harvey thought? He sat as still as possible and clutched the baby tighter to his chest.

The approaching car came to a stop and a very tall and well-dressed woman slid from the driver's seat and headed toward the police car, her hands clearly out in the open. Here was a woman who understood the situation. She walked with long and affirmative strides. Her long black wool coat blew open in a breeze and she wrapped it tightly around herself against the cold.

Pete seemed to size her up fully and then stepped out of the shadows to ask, "Are you with CPS?"

"Yes," she replied. "My name is Roberta McEniry. And your name?"

"I'm Officer Pete Murdock of the Port Orchard police force." He seemed to relax a bit and nodded towards the car. "Come with me. The child is in here with the man who found her, Harvey Waggoner."

In the car, Harvey was doing his best to turn around and watch what was going on without waking Anna. As he observed the woman get out of the car and walk toward the SUV, he was struck by her confidence. She was not anything he imagined the CPS people would be like. She was tall, downright good looking, and seemed to carry a ton of authority.

Then he thought *she is going to take Anna.* That thought made Harvey very anxious and oddly possessive of the tiny girl.

Roberta opened the door next to where Harvey was sitting and introduced herself. "I'm the person in charge of Child Protective Services for Pierce County. I'm here to pick up this little girl and take her into protective custody," she whispered.

"Anna," Harvey said sharply. "Her name is Anna."

Roberta stood with a sincere smile. She did not make any move toward the baby. She had seen this before. A stranger saves a child from a very bad situation and then develops a connection. Situations like this are very sensitive for the caregiver and the child. Throughout her years of experience, she found it was sometimes difficult for the rescuers to let go of a wounded child. It was almost as if they assumed the parental role.

Standing very still so as to not invade his space, Roberta asked, "May I ask your name, sir?"

"Harvey. Harvey Waggoner"

Roberta leaned in a little and quietly asked, "Harvey, can you tell me what happened here? Can you tell me how you ended up with this child?"

Harvey went through the story again for Roberta as he had already done several times for the police. She continued to stand outside, never making a move to take the child, and listened with intense concentration to show she was more concerned about Anna than anything else at this moment.

"Has she been physically hurt as far as you can tell?" Roberta asked.

"I only changed her diapers and put on a new pair of pants since she was covered in, you know, poo-poo, when I arrived. I haven't looked anywhere else on her body," Harvey responded. "But I've got to say, I don't know what she's been through, but I know it must have been horrifying. She's even lost her voice from screaming so much. Who knows how long she was in that back seat alone before I drove up? Who knows what happened to her mother in the front seat? Who knows what this child may have witnessed?

"I can assure you that Officer Murdock and I will get to the bottom of this," stated Roberta. "I consider myself an expert when it comes to unwinding terrible situations for children. I do this every day. I will take every precaution to not alarm or distress this child any more than necessary. I feel a deep compassion for infants who have no defense mechanism or the ability to understand anything but being loved or living in fear. Please trust me, Mr. Waggoner, I will take good care of this child and she will be in a home that will protect and love her until this is all sorted out."

Just then Anna woke up smiling at Harvey. He smiled back at her calling her by name and holding her tightly. *Oh my,* he thought, *this child is depending on me to protect her.*

As Roberta took a step in to take Anna, the baby screamed, with what little voice she had left. Anna's eyes opened wide in panic, and she grabbed Harvey's shirt and held on for dear life.

"Wait a minute, wait a minute," shouted Harvey. "I've got a better idea."

"Mr. Waggoner," Roberta said calmly as she backed off a little, "you're only making this worse for the child."

"What if I go with you to wherever you're going to take her? Then she'll only need one more transfer of hands," pleaded Harvey.

"Mr. Waggoner, I'm sorry, but that just can't happen. There are laws and rules that must be followed for the safety and well-being of the child," stated Roberta.

"I get that. I'm an attorney. I know all about laws and rules," he said with a testy, pleading voice. "What about this then? Let me at least carry her to your car and put her in the car seat?" He was doing everything to hang on to this little baby until the moment he just had to let her go.

What am I doing? He screamed at himself inside his head. *What am I doing here? This is nuts.*

He and Roberta stared at each other for a moment. Harvey held Anna tight against his chest as Roberta gave him a not unkind scowl. Just then, they both caught the odor of messy diapers. Roberta relaxed a bit and said with a small sigh, "Okay, you can take her to the car, but that may be even worse for you."

Roberta McEniry was not just a worker with the CPS; she was the head of the service for the three counties with her main office in Pierce County. She was a very visible and strong-willed social worker. Roberta's reputation was known by most anyone in the CPS system and the state.

She was tough. She had a great head on her shoulders, and she loved her job. She had worked with the Juvenile Court for decades and ran a very tight ship in the counties she was responsible for. She had previously been married to a Superior Court Judge who had served his assignment in Juvenile Court in Pierce County, but he hated every minute of it. He hated his marriage almost as much, so Roberta chose to continue working with the children.

She was compassionate, detailed oriented, determined, and possessed the tenacity of a terrier to get what she thought was fair and in the best interest of the child. She had gone many rounds with defending attorneys, who were furnished by the courts to represent the parents in their abuse and abandonment cases. Roberta demanded proof, solid proof that the parents were equipped with all they needed to take care of the children. She would make sure they had everything available to help them be better parents, but they had to do the actual work. If they didn't do what was ordered by the court, or if they didn't work harder than ever to get their kid back, then she would make sure the child was matched with the best foster home.

Roberta understood, sometimes painfully, that the mandate of the state is to return the child to the parents. She agreed that this was often the right thing to do not only for the parents but more especially for the children. But she also knew there were plenty of times when she had no option but to return the children even though she knew the parents were lying to the courts or using someone else's

BROKEN TRUST: CHILDREN IN PERIL

urine to pass urinalyses or other drug tests. Those were the cases where she fought the most and she never gave a child up without a fight. She had earned the nickname, 'Jaguar', one of the most dangerous cats on the planet. Just like the real jaguars in the forest, the real danger wasn't when you crossed the cat, but when you crossed it on its turf. The jaguar is a vicious killer for their size, dragging its prey down and then suffocating it. It is also stealthy and adaptable.

Roberta knew about her nickname. She had heard opponents and colleagues refer to her by that moniker many times in the break room after a big court day where everyone was rehashing what had occurred. She knew she had many characteristics of her nickname animal, but she took it as a sign of admiration and respect, not as an intended slam by the department.

If a Social Worker didn't do his or her job properly, Roberta was known to jump right into the middle of the case. No one wanted that because not only did it not look good on that Social Worker's record, but they would certainly not enjoy the ride for the rest of the case.

It was not unusual for Roberta to go on a referral and pick up a child who had been hurt or abandoned. This task was usually done by others in her department, but she loved keeping her boots on the ground so she would never lose touch with the nightmares that the children suffered.

On this particular night, she had been working late at the office on cases she was closing, when the incident was called in on the police scanner. The situation had piqued her interest and she wasn't ready to go home to a lonely house just yet. She called the social worker on duty and told her not to worry about it and she would catch up and pass off the case later. The location was in her backyard anyway.

20

She never wanted to feel she had been in the office environment for too long and that she was losing her edge on being able to relate with these trauma-ridden kids. She had seen so many children abused in so many unthinkable ways, it turned her stomach. Above that, there was the devastation it would have on their entire lives. Here was a way of contributing at least something and seeing the case from the very beginning.

Once she heard the call come in on the scanner, she waited until the call came in from the field, and then headed out to the site where the child had been found.

CHAPTER 4

ARVEY SLEPT IN LATE THE NEXT DAY. HE HAD NOT gotten home until after 3AM and was exhausted from the time change, the intense work he had done in Chicago, and of course the excitement of the previous night.

Harvey woke up around noon, then slowly got out of bed and opened the drapes. He had closed them when he got home, not wanting to wake up with the sun glaring in his bedroom. As he opened his eyes, he could see there was a cloud cover and threat of rain on the horizon, but it was brilliantly beautiful. This was what he loved about the Pacific Northwest and about his home on the Puget Sound in Port Orchard

Unbidden, his mind wandered to the events of the last night and especially to Anna. He felt his stomach tighten from worry about where she had ended up. He wondered if she had been able to calm down or if she was still crying. With an effort, he forced himself to put those thoughts aside in his mind and get up and start his weekend. He knew he had to stop this obsessive worry about a child he knew nothing about.

Harvey showered and got dressed in casual pants and a sweater, his normal attire on lazy weekends. As he stared in the mirror, looking at himself, he was reminded how fortunate he had been in his life. He was a reasonably good-looking man with a good education, a great job, and good friends that would do anything for him. He had loved and lost, but he had been able to transfer all those emotions into his work. He could not stop thinking about the woman in the car who had been beaten by someone, possibly even Anna's dad. He knew that he would be dwelling on his sorrow for the entire weekend.

He walked over to the top of his dresser and rummaged through his keys and change, trying to find Pete Murdock's business card. He would *call* Pete him to see how things were with Anna and the lady. He knew they would be calling him soon enough to come in to give an official statement but he didn't want to wait any longer.

Before he could dig out the card, the front doorbell rang. He opened the door to find stood Officer Pete standing with two men dressed in suits. "Officer Pete, I was just about to give you a call," said Harvey.

"Harvey, these are Detective Robert James and Detective Martin Cowell. Can we come in and talk for a few minutes?"

"Of course," replied Harvey. "Please come in and have a seat."

As the three law enforcement officers walked into Harvey's family room, they were greeted with a floor to ceiling glass window exposing the beautiful waters of Puget Sound. It was clear they were impressed, despite the seriousness of their demeanors.

"Can I offer you some coffee?" Harvey asked. "I'm getting myself a cup."

"No, thank you," Pete replied for all three of them men as they sat down facing the view.

"Rather than dragging you down to the station on Saturday," said Pete, "we decided to come to you."

Harvey fixed himself a coffee in his Keurig coffee maker and turned around and said, "I would have been happy to come there, but I'm glad you came out. I missed out on a lot of sleep last night, just like you."

"We have some news I wanted you to hear from us before reading it in the paper" said Pete as his head and voice dropped down.

Pete took a deep breath and continued. "That WAS Anna's mom in the car last night. We're assuming her boyfriend, who could be Anna's dad, was the one who did the beating."

"How is Anna?" Harvey asked quickly.

"I'm not sure," replied Pete. "It's not our job to follow that through. Once CPS has control of the child, we're out of it, unless we're needed later on for some reason."

Pete continued trying to get out what he wanted to say before Harvey could interrupt further. "But I wanted you to know that this is no longer just an abuse case. I'm sorry to tell you that the woman died this morning about two hours after we got her to the hospital. She never regained consciousness, so she couldn't tell us what actually happened. Her attacker hit her in the face, and beat her up so badly as well as using his knife to cut her, that she was beyond recognition. The beating also damaged the brain so badly it created a clot. We're desperately looking for any next of kin. But in these cases where the parent has fallen so far, most of all the relatives have either been exhausted with helping or are nowhere to be found. We've been in contact with Ms. McEniry from CPS, you may remember meeting her, and she's pulling out all stops to help place Anna."

Harvey's face drained of color as he heard this news. He put his coffee cup down and slid back in his chair. All he could think of was how this defenseless little baby must have suffered, having a strung-out mom and no home, and then witnessing the beating and murder of her mother.

"We've confirmed that the woman was at our station late yesterday saying her boyfriend was trying to kill her." Pete looked apologetic as he continued, "There is only so much we can do without proof and, honestly, she was such a mess. We had no idea at the time if she was high or just crazy.

"No excuses, but yesterday was an extremely busy day for the station. We were short-staffed and we're a small station anyway. But we should have tried harder. We just had nothing to base her claim on. She had no permanent address, no one to call, no place to stay. Apparently, she and Anna were living in her car. We had no one at the station to sit down with her and try to get to the bottom of her claim. I'm sorry, but we just let her walk out," confessed Officer Pete. "You have no idea how bad we feel about this, but we were following protocol."

"There's more," Pete continued, drooping still further in his seat. "When we picked up the car last night and took it to the garage, out officers pulled the back seat out and found several blocks of Heroin, some Fentanyl, and four AK-47 semiautomatic rifles."

"What?" Harvey squeaked in alarm. "Are you saying the mom was in the drug business with Anna in the back seat?"

"No, we don't think so," Pete firmly stated. "We do suspect, however, that her boyfriend must have stashed the goods in the car, and in the heat of whatever happened he forgot or was going to come back and get it later. Or possibly he got interrupted by someone else before he could get the contraband out. With this amount of drugs and guns, and how they were packed in the car, it looks like whoever is doing this is a small-time guy dealing drugs in our county. But the thing we've learned is that where there's a small-time dealer, there's also a big fish buying and pushing mountains of illegal drugs. We've been seeing a lot of this lately.

"There were additional fresh tire tracks that were almost side by side with the mom's car," Pete explained. "From the size and imprint of the tires, it looks like a big truck. We're not sure how all this plays out, but something went down, and it wasn't just beating up a woman leaving her unconscious with a crying baby in the back seat. We don't even know if what happened last night is related to the mom's visit to the station or what she was trying to tell anyone. Based on identification from cameras at the station and the plates on the car, we were able to pull up an expired driver's license for the woman. So at least we have somewhere to start."

CHAPTER 5

HARVEY WAS TRYING TO WRAP HIS HEAD AROUND ALL this discussion with the detectives when his cell phone rang. He looked down at the number and didn't recognize it, so he ignored the ringing.

"Anna's mother is dead?" asked Harvey in shocked disbelief. "Where is Anna? What's going to happen to Anna? Is that killer dad going to get Anna back? You've got to tell me where Anna is. She's all alone in this world now. Who's going to love that child?"

His cell phone rang and vibrated again on the coffee table. Harvey didn't even bother to look. He was too overwhelmed with sadness.

Pete spoke as calmly as he could, knowing Harvey was as upset now as he had been the evening before. "Harvey, these detectives want to ask you some questions. This is now a murder investigation, not just domestic violence and abandonment of an infant, although that's bad enough! Do you mind answering their questions?"

Harvey shook his head. "No… yes, of course I will, but you were there. You know as much as I do. More, actually."

"You may have seen things, little things that you may not recall that could be important to this investigation," explained the policeman

Again, the cell phone rang and vibrated. Harvey picked it up in anger, barking out an annoyed "Hello."

"Mr. Waggoner," a voice said kindly. "This is Roberta McEniry from Child Protective Services."

Harvey jumped off the couch like he had been shot. "Oh, Ms. McEniry, thank you so much for calling me. Can you please tell me how Anna is doing? I just heard the news about her mother. In fact, the police are here now," Harvey explained his tone much gentler. "I apologize for my rudeness when I answered I'd just been told about Anna's mother. I really am sorry. I'm better than that. I've just been so very concerned about the little girl."

"That's fine, Mr. Waggoner," replied Roberta, sounding like she was smiling. "Listen, I called because I knew you would want to know about Anna. She's doing much better and has already been placed in a really good foster home. Roberta went on in a reassuring tone, "She was perfect on the ride back to my office where we stayed for a while until I found the perfect spot for her earlier this morning. I took her to this wonderful home and while she tried to cry a little, even though her voice is still shot, she appeared not as traumatized as she was last night. Just so you know, Mr. Waggoner, the foster mom, held her tight and sang to her until she stopped whimpering. I stayed around for a while to make sure Anna was going to adjust. The foster mom gave her a warm bath and bottle. By the time I left,

Anna was sound asleep in her crib. She had a full belly, a clean body, and she was warm and safe."

Now more relaxed, Harvey excused himself for a moment from the guests on his couch and walked into the kitchen. "Ms. McEniry," Harvey began.

She responded immediately. "Please call me Roberta. I mean we do have each other's business cards, right?" she chuckled. They had traded business cards when Harvey placed Anna in her car. He wanted this CPS person to have his card and know how to reach him and he certainly wanted to know how to reach her.

Harvey laughed in return, "I was just going to say how happy I am that we exchanged cards last night because you were my next call when the police left. Thank you for letting me know how things are going. Can I go see Anna?"

"I'm afraid not, Harvey. That's against policy, I'm afraid."

"But I really need to see her," Harvey pleaded. I feel like I am responsible for her in some weird way. I don't know how to explain, but I feel she and I had a connection somehow. I don't have children, but somehow, we bonded. I really believe she may need me."

"She needed you last night, Harvey," Roberta stated firmly but kindly. "She needed you the most when you were there. Don't forget that. Officer Pete told me how you calmed her down by singing 'Cat's in the Cradle' to her. He told me how tender you were in changing her soiled diapers and how you called her by name over and over, giving her the assurance of the only thing she knew. How did you know, anyway?" she asked.

"How did I know what? 'Cat's in the Cradle?'"

"No, silly, to call her by name. That's very important in traumas, especially in infants. That was brilliant for a non-child attorney!" said Roberta.

"You know," said Harvey, "I'm not sure how or even if I knew. I just knew if I were in some kind of distress and I had no control, I would want someone calling my name!"

"Well, it's right out of the handbook, I'll tell you that. Good job, Harvey!"

Harvey sat for a moment in silence, basking in the compliment and wondering how he could have known how to respond. Before he could respond, he was shocked when Officer Pete tapped him on the shoulder. Harvey had forgotten that Pete and the others were even there.

"Sorry to interrupt, Harvey, but we really need to talk with you. These guys need to get on this case before it gets cold." Pete stated.

Harvey held up one finger. "I'll be right there. Give me one minute."

"Roberta" said Harvey into the phone, "I need to go now. But may I call you back so I can find out more about what Anna is going through?"

"Yes, of course you can. Let me give you my personal cell number." She gave him the number and then continued, "Harvey, the law is very clear on how much I can reveal to you. Honestly, I am not supposed to even acknowledge that there is a case, or that an Anna Taylor even exists, for that matter. But I realize these are unusual circumstances and I will keep you as updated as I can. Just don't expect miracles like being able to go see her."

Thank you again for calling. I'll give you a call soon," Harvey said, hanging up the phone with a smile. He returned to the family room where Pete and the two detectives were waiting and chatting about possibilities for this crime.

Harvey grabbed his coffee and sat back in his seat as the questioning began. He hated reviewing the horror of the last night's event. He felt he was reliving it over again, feeling the tug of Anna on his shirt when Roberta arrived at the car to pick her up. He tried to listen to the detectives' questions, but he was lost in thought as he wondered what was going to happen to this baby now that her mother was dead.

They questioned him for about an hour until they got up to leave. Just as they were about to leave, Harvey shouted, "Holy crap! I forgot to pick up Velcro at the kennels. I need to get out of here." He grabbed his coat and escorted his guests out the door.

Velcro was an Australian Shepherd named Velcro that Harvey had gotten after his wife died and he moved to Washington. He had needed company, and the little pup did the job. She was smart, loyal, and almost intuitive as to what he was going to do. Harvey loved this dog with all of his heart. Velcro always did her part protecting the place and when Harvey was home, you could find Velcro right at his heels. She never let him out of her sight.

In all the excitement since returning early this morning from the crime scene, he had forgotten all about her. He hustled the policemen out of his house then jumped in his car, which still smelled Anna's old blanket, heading to the kennels where Velcro had become a favorite guest of the owners.

Despite the delayed pick-up, the homecoming was what it always was when Harvey came back from a trip. Velcro was beside herself loving, licking, and getting as close to her master as she could. On the way back, Harvey decided he was hungry and drove through a fast-food place to get him a burger and fries, and, of course, a little burger for Velcro. When he reached the turn off to his house, which was about 50 yards down a gravel driveway, shielded from the street by hedges and trees, he passed a car on the side of the road. The vehicle looked out of place to him, and before he turned into the driveway, he looked in his rearview mirror and saw two greasy looking characters smoking cigarettes and watching him. He turned his blinker off and kept driving straight ahead toward the curve that would take him back around, a route that only a local would know about.

As he slowly edged around the corner, he took his phone out and snapped a picture just before he turned into his driveway.

Rough and seedy looking as they were, the two guys in the car were certainly not selling Girl Scout Cookies. Just as he turned in, they took off and whizzed past him, as if firing a warning shot across his bow.

CHAPTER 6

HARVEY QUICKLY GATHERED HIS FOOD AND HEADED into the house, calling Velcro to follow. Velcro was so happy to be home that she ran all through the house barking and playing with every toy in each of the rooms.

Harvey dropped his fast-food bags on the table in the kitchen which looked out on Puget Sound. Even though he was alarmed by the men in the car, he felt blessed to live in such a beautiful place. It was late afternoon, but the water sparkled as if diamonds were just below the surface. In the distance he could see clouds rolling in, but after all, this was the Northwest. Rain is a common thing. New as he was in the area, he was beginning to get used to the changeable weather.

He made a mental note to call his new friend Pete and send him the photo of the car's license plate. He wondered if they might have just been casing the place for a burglary. His house was out of the way and he had read in the local newspaper of several recent break-ins in his little town.

He was suddenly overwhelmed by the feeling of being in his comfortable home with Velcro playing at his feet. His mind wandered back to how he had felt the first night he stayed there after moving in. Cassie had only been gone for a few months, and he remembered how he just had to get out of the city. He felt like he was suffering from claustrophobia… like the walls were closing in and the city was crippling for him.

He and his late wife had met at Columbia Law School where they became good buddies but not a thing. They reconnected years later when they ended up at the same large law firm in New York years later. Cassie was an interesting woman. She came from big money on the east coast and never lacked anything. Her family had a house in the Hamptons, a ranch in Montana, and who knows where else? But regardless of her "silver spoon" upbringing, she was engaging, warm, smart, funny, beautiful, and just this side of crazy. That was what attracted him to her so quickly when they met up again in New York, that slightly wild and crazy part of her that was always in charge. She was so free and bold, a huge risk taker, doing things other attorneys didn't have the courage to do. She could bluff her way better than the more established attorneys whose careers were based on that one skill.

At first, they were just old law school friends going out and having a drink or taking in a show. But without warning from each of them, they fell in love. They fell so hard and so fast that within months they flew off to Las Vegas and got married. Cassie's parents were furious since she was expected to have a huge wedding in the Hamptons or at the best hotel in New York City. Harvey and Cassie didn't care; they were in love.

Over time, it was clear the two personalities clashed more than they hummed. They were constantly fighting over the smallest of things. Cassie became unbearable, and Harvey did everything he could to keep things together.

About six years into their marriage, Cassie came home and, without any warning, told Harvey she had a very rare form of aggressive breast cancer. That night the walls started closing in on Harvey. Even though they had both discussed a divorce, this was not what Harvey had expected. Cassie didn't deserve this death sentence. Harvey and Cassie had both agreed they had "fallen out of love," but they were still best friends at heart. He went to work every day, trying to keep up with his case load, and still take care of Cassie as she continued treatments, but it was becoming a difficult task for Harvey to remain the strong support person he needed to be for his wife.

The pain, suffering and agony lasted about eighteen months. Two weeks before her fortieth birthday, Cassie passed away in the predawn beauty of the early morning.

Harvey was devastated. He had no idea what to do without her. Her presence was everywhere; he felt her at home, in the gym, at the office, and especially when seeing their friends. He had months where he would only sleep for no more than an hour. His work suffered, as did his personal relationships. He could not seem to get a grip on his life. He began to hate the city and even the job he loved dearly at one time.

One late Friday night while Harvey was still at the office, he got a call from one of the largest corporate law firms in Seattle. They wanted to fly him out to see if he would be a fit for their team. At first, Harvey thought it was a lousy idea, but the more he got to thinking about it, the more he liked the idea of getting out of New York.

He wanted a fresh start, but did he want to trade one big city for another? Then he remembered something Cassie always told him; there is only one Big City and that's New York!

Harvey flew out to Seattle the following weekend and was overwhelmed by the beauty of the mountains and the Puget Sound waterways. The old songs were true. The bluest skies you'll ever see are in Seattle. The firm's offices were right downtown, which was beautiful too, but he decided to negotiate working from a home office several days a week. He wanted to change everything about his life.

Harvey's reputation as a corporate attorney was stellar. He had led high-profile cases in New York involving some of the city's and the world's biggest organizations. He figured that gave him a little bit of an edge here to get the few things he wanted in his life now.

It took a couple of months and some hard negotiating (he even pulled a few of Cassie's tricks during the negotiation stage), but Harvey made the deal. Off to Seattle he went looking for some room to breathe and a new lifestyle. He shopped for real estate for weeks, looking at all the places recommended by the law firm as upscale communities.

One afternoon after picking up his new SUV, he decided he would take the ferry and explore. He had no idea where he was headed; he just hopped the ferry with the shortest line of cars. As the boat took off, he made his way to the upper deck and looked back at his new city. He was awestruck at the beauty and the majesty of the mountain range on the horizon. He could not feel any freer than he did at that moment. He wanted that view to be a part of his daily life. As it ended up, he was on the ferry to Port Orchard.

He followed the small crowd off the boat and soon found himself driving around the most captivating community he had ever seen. All at once, he felt like he could breathe again, more lighthearted than he had felt since before Cassie and he had gotten married. The place was gorgeous, and there were plenty of restaurants, shops, and even fast-food drive-ups for late night eating. There were medical clinics, although he was glad that part of his life had gone for now, as well as plenty of veterinarians, public schools, and every service he could imagine. Harvey got so excited he decided he pulled into one of the burger places and got something to eat.

As hungry as he was excited, Harvey pulled into one of the burger places to grab something to eat. As he pulled out of the drive-thru biting into the burger, he thought *this is really one of the best burgers I've ever had!* He kept driving, trying to get closer to the water. He had been driving around about an hour when he spotted the Sound from the road he was on. He also saw a for-sale sign along the side closest to the water.

He slowly pulled up to the driveway and peered through the opening, his heart pounding with excitement. He got out of the car and pulled out one of the realty flyers from the box on the sign. Apparently, the house was vacant since he didn't see anyone around and there were no cars in the driveway. The building looked as if it could use some work, but oh, the view!

Harvey picked up his phone and called his realtor in Seattle and told her what he'd found. She had worked with most of the attorneys in the firm and knew the area well. She told Harvey that Port Orchard was too far a commute and tried to talk him out of it with all of the persuasive logic she could muster. Her arguments were hopeless. He was intent on buying the house in Port Orchard.

"I want to put an offer in today", Harvey told his agent.

"Today?" she squealed. "You haven't even seen the inside yet and the owners will need to be contacted."

"No" said Harvey, "the place is vacant. I'm standing in the back yard looking at this amazing view. My mind is made up."

"Mr. Waggoner, if you're looking for a view, the houses we looked at on Mercer Island are far more applicable for your new position at the firm," the Realtor firmly stated.

"I'm sorry, I don't care about your opinion as to whether this is 'applicable to the firm. 'This is the house I want, and this is where I'm making an offer today, with or without you."

A few weeks later, after a ton of repairs and upgrades, Harvey moved in his boxes. He had to purchase everything because he had left most of his belongings in New York. Cassie's mother wanted the photos and wall art. Cassie's sister wanted the very expensive furniture and other items Cassie had purchased. All Harvey brought was his clothes, some law books, and a few personal items from their marriage. While the repairs and upgrades were going on, Harvey bought a bedroom set and hired a decorator to buy furniture for the rest of the house. He had to hire someone for the lawn upkeep and find a handy man he could call on regularly, since he was never good with anything that required tools.

As the moving truck left, he stood at the entrance of his new life looking out at the most beautiful scenery he had ever seen. Oh, he and Cassie had been all around Europe and there were some beautiful spots he had seen. But this spot was his. This was something he could wake up to every day. He had never been so content and happy. He was finding it hard to believe he was even here.

The first evening closed in, with nothing for him to do but watch some television. He didn't have to be at work at the office until next week, and although he knew they were already lining up some cases for him to start with, he had a long weekend left before he was expected to jump in gear.

Just then he suffered the largest pang of loneliness he had ever felt. He even missed the quarreling with Cassie and tried to remember those times and how cagey and smart she was as she out foxed half of the partners at the firm. He wanted to remember those good memories and not the last two years when she was so sick and in so much pain.

Then an idea came to him. He knew exactly what he needed to get started in my new home. He whipped out his phone and started looking up pet shelters. He needed a dog!

CHAPTER 7

HARVEY CLIMBED INTO HIS NEW VEHICLE, WHICH HE absolutely loved, and tried to input the address into the car's GPS system. It took him a while, but he finally got his directions working and drove up the circular drive to the road.

He surprised himself at how quickly he was finding his way around his new home. The signs on the roads were good and it seemed like an easy little town to navigate. He was just enjoying this perfect day in his perfect new life.

It just so happened that the day before his arrival, the shelter he located had received a small litter of puppies. They were about four months old. The pups were primarily Australian Shepherds, dropped off as the owner was moving overseas and didn't have time to get rid of the dogs in any other way. Harvey walked back to the viewing area looking at all the dogs, thinking how they all needed good homes. Then he saw Her and they made eye contact. She was in a cage with her brothers or sisters. They all looked alike except she had a round black spot on her white ear. He felt an instant connection.

"That's the one I want, right there, Harvey told the attendant The puppy sat upright as if to say, "I'm ready, let's go." *This dog is silly smart*, Harvey thought.

Harvey went through all the necessary paperwork, background checks, etc. and then took her home a couple of hours later. She sat in the front seat like a grown up, just watching her new owner and being so darn cute!

The first night, she was into everything that wasn't tied down. She was unquestionably a puppy. Harvey kept investigating "Google" to learn how to train puppies, then going back to the dog and trying out the things he had learned. Everything she got into would seem to stick to her coat, or on her mouth, or at her tail. She proudly came out of the bedroom with a sock stuck to her back. Somehow, she had dried leaves stuck to her mouth. She was like a magnet. Without a moment of doubt, Harvey said, "Okay, let's name you Velcro!"

That night when they were headed to bed, Harvey opened the crate he had brought for her and put in his bedroom. After getting ready for bed and just before he got in bed, he said to Velcro, "Come one girl, get in your bed." Velcro looked at him like he had just stepped off Mars. "Come on girl, get into bed now", Harvey repeated, using his firm voice.

Velcro just sat there looking at him for a moment then ran to a box next to the bed and jumped up. She immediately went to the foot and went to sleep.

Harvey thought, *well dang, it'd be nice to have someone in bed with me.* Harvey slid into the bed and was quickly asleep. Velcro, knowing he was sleeping, walked softly up to him and nudged herself right near his chest. Harvey opened his eyes, seeing his new sleeping mate, patted her on the head and said, "Velcro, you better not pee on my bed or anywhere else for that matter." Velcro closed her eyes and they both fell asleep.

The sun came in the window early on a Saturday and woke up Harvey. He still loved every minute looking at the blue skies or even the rain. He never felt so free. He didn't have to wake up surrounded by tall buildings and honking horns. As soon as he moved, Velcro jumped up and barked and barked. Harvey quickly looked at the bed and the floor to see if there had been an accident, but Velcro was in the clear.

Then Harvey remembered, *oh yeah, I should let her outside.* Velcro beat him to the door and quickly ran outside into the back yard and did her business before bounding back to the door where Harvey was waiting for her. He thought to himself, *how did she know to do that? She's only four months old.* But it seemed that Velcro seemed to catch on to things really quickly. It was almost as if he only had to tell her once and she would fall in line.

From that day forward, they were inseparable whenever Harvey was home. Her presence was one more reason why he was so thrilled that he had negotiated to work from home frequently. It allowed him more time to enjoy his new life, his new home, and his new best friend.

• • •

On the Sunday after the harrowing morning that he had found Anna, Harvey and Velcro slept in later than usual. Usually, on Sundays, he was up early getting work done so he could have the afternoon to play around the house or go to a movie or go have brunch somewhere. Some Sundays he thought about going to the little church just down the road. Church was in his upbringing, although at some point he had left that in the past. In the backwash of Cassie's death and all that came after, he never lost sight of knowing there is a God and that Jesus died for him. He wasn't one to talk about it much and it had been years since he had really been involved in a church. There was even a stretch with Cassie that he didn't go to church at all. Cassie thought it was a waste of time.

Harvey went in to brew himself a cup of coffee. Anna came flooding to his mind and he wondered how she was doing in her new home. He thought he should give Roberta a call. He had taken a liking to the CPS worker. She was gentle, kind, and obviously good at her job. He wanted somehow to convince her to let him see Anna in her new environment, although he knew it was unlikely. In the back of his mind, he could tell he kind of liked Roberta as a woman as well. She was a looker, for sure. He shook his head and said, "Stop that, Harvey!"

As he munched on his late breakfast, he was bothered by something but couldn't quite pin down. Then he had a flashback of the two thugs sitting in a car in front of his place. Oh yeah, Harvey thought to himself as he let Velcro back inside. *I need to call Pete and let him know there may be potential burglars in the area.*

After getting showered and dressed, he decided it was time to take Velcro for a long walk. He could use the exercise to clear his head. He had been putting in the hours lately, working a case that was just about to break open and probably end up in court. He knew that the work was going to suck up huge amounts of his time, so he had better get some enjoyment while he could.

As he and Velcro headed up the driveway to the road, Harvey spotted a familiar car sitting across the road. He took his phone out of its holder and pulled up the picture he had taken yesterday. It was the same car. Uncertain what to do, he made his right turn on to the road, leaving the suspicious car in his rearview mirror.

Harvey felt unsure what was going on but decided to double back and see if they were still there. As he took the circle shortcut and slowly turned on to his street behind where the car had been, he saw the car still parked at the opening of his hedges with two guys looking down the drive at his house. When someone behind him honked since he was driving so slowly, he sped up just as the car pulled away from his driveway entrance.

For a moment he thought, *I'm going to follow these guys.* Then logic and caution set in. Those two were probably just casing his house for a burglary. He should let the professionals take care of that.

He looked over at Velcro in the front seat with her doggie seat belt attached and said, "You know what, girl? We're going to make a short stop before we go to do our walk." Velcro barked one time as if to answer, *whatever you say dude. I'm with you!*

Harvey wasn't far from the police station, so he pulled up in front. He reached over and unhooked Velcro and they stepped out of the car.

As he entered the station, he was greeted by a very nice young lady with a big smile saying, "Welcome to Port Orchard Police Department, what I can do for you today, sir?"

Harvey thought, *I know this is a small town now. In New York, when you enter a police station, no one ever calls you 'sir' and they certainly don't ask how they can help you.* He returned the smile and introduced himself and Velcro and asked for Pete Murdock.

"I'm sorry, sir, Officer Murdock is not on duty today. Can someone else help you or can I leave him a message for you?" she kindly responded.

Remembering the other two detectives who visited him on Saturday were from Tacoma, Harvey declined and said he would contact him tomorrow.

"Are you sure no one else can help? We have a couple of other officers here in the station," she asked.

"No thanks, I'll give Pete a call tomorrow. It's not that important."

As Harvey and Velcro turned to walk out the door, the charming greeter said, "Have a blessed day, Mr. Waggoner and you too, Velcro."

"Blessed day?" Harvey said aloud when he had gone out the door. "Who says have a 'blessed' day? Wow! I am living in Hooterville," he chuckled, heading for the car.

After the pleasant interaction, he was in a great mood as he and Velcro headed out for their long walk. After the walk and a stop for a milk shake at his favorite hamburger drive-thru, he and Velcro headed home. The events of the day had melted away in the fresh salt air and the beautiful weather. Crisp, sunny, water, blue skies…ah, he thought it just could not get better.

When he arrived home, Velcro barked entering the front door as she always did to say she was glad to be home. Harvey felt the same way.

He flipped on a basketball game and grabbed a bag of popcorn, deciding to rest a little before he dove into work. He did not even know what teams were playing as he settled in for just a few minutes.

He dozed off and was awakened by the vibration of his cell phone. He grabbed the phone, looking to see who was calling and was surprised to see it was Roberta.

"Hi ya, Roberta," Harvey asked with a lift in his voice. "It's good to hear from you."

"Harvey, I have some bad news," Roberta said, her voice all professional business. "Remember what I told you about the fact that I can't share information with you because you're not part of the 'case?'"

He responded quickly with a little laugh, "Yes, I was going to talk to you about that after I investigated a way to rewrite the rules and regulations so I could see Anna. Is Anna still doing okay in her foster home?"

Roberta answered, "I'm afraid not. Anna has been admitted to the hospital."

CHAPTER 8

HARVEY'S GOOD MOOD VANISHED IN AN INSTANT. "Please, Roberta, tell me what happened," he pleaded. He was more upset than he realized he'd be. The last time he saw the baby, she was smiling and pulling his heartstrings. Somehow, he felt that he let her down.

"It's hard to say for sure," Roberta explained, "but the doctors think she came in contact with fentanyl, possibly through her skin. After we spoke yesterday, I got a call from the foster mom saying she was at the hospital with Anna. Since she knew there had been violence involved with Anna's mom somehow – by the way, we keep our foster parents in the dark too. It's not just you, it's the law.

"The foster mom noticed that Anna was having difficulty breathing. She had thrown up in her sleep and wouldn't eat. Mostly she was gasping for breath. The mom knew she had cried a lot and had lost her voice, but she thought she might have come down with 'flu or possibly pneumonia. To be on the safe side, she took her to the emergency room at Mary Bridge Children's Hospital in Tacoma.

When she arrived, Anna was unconscious and later it was determined she's in a coma."

Harvey could feel the tears welling up in his eyes, although he had never been a crier. He remembered feeling the tug on his shirt that night when Anna was trying to hang on to him when anyone new approached. He remembered how she slept so heavily in his arms. All the sights and sounds came flooding back and he was so upset he could hardly think of what question to ask next.

Roberta continued, "The police were called, and the detectives came to the hospital after tests were run, discovering she had fentanyl in her bloodstream. The doctors also did an x-ray of her legs because they noticed bruises on her body. It was discovered that she had fractures in both legs. According to how you found her that night, locked in her car seat, they don't believe the injury was from an accident. It seems more likely she was dropped or hit as there were many old fractures. The police told the doctors how we found her and advised them that this is a murder case because of the mother's death. The protocol is that when any abuse is noticed, the hospital is required to notify the social worker immediately. Since there has been no social worker assigned yet, I got the call.

"As for the fentanyl, I'm told it's only a trace amount, but there's enough exposure to put Anna in jeopardy. I know how toxic and dangerous the drug can be, especially to an infant," said Roberta.

There was a long silence at the other end of the phone, and then Harvey quietly asked, "What do you mean jeopardy? Do you mean she may die?"

"I'm not a doctor, Harvey. I'm just giving you the facts as I know them. The doctors are very concerned at this point and, well, I guess all we can do is wait to hear."

Harvey could hardly believe what he had heard. Why didn't he see bruising on Anna when he changed the diaper in the back of his car? Did he hold her too tightly, hurting her broken leg seven more? He was sick to his stomach.

Breaking the long silence, Roberta said, "Harvey, I overheard the detectives talking outside the room. They seem to have a person pinpointed for involvement or potential involvement, and I heard something about a Mexican connection."

"Roberta, I have to say, the best thing about any of this is that you are on the case for Anna. I trust you completely. And I'm an attorney who generally doesn't trust anyone," Harvey stated. "Can I please come and see her in the hospital?"

"Tell you what," she replied with compassion for his pleading. "Why don't you come and run into me by accident when I happen to be standing near Anna's room. If the coast is clear, you can at least see her. The foster mom is still with her most of the time. But we can work something out. Can we synchronize our schedules? I don't want you to miss out on an opportunity to see her."

They agreed to meet up the next evening around 7 PM. "Roberta," said Harvey. "I'm very thankful to have met you. If I had to be the one to discover this mess, then I believe it was meant to be that way. Having you show up when you could have sent someone else was a true blessing. I also want you to know I do have a few connections here in Washington State and I'm going to make some calls to see if I can find out the scoop on what's really going on with this case."

"Thank you for the kind words, Harvey. If I had to be involved in something this complex, I'm glad you're the person I'm dealing with."

They hung up with Harvey's mood now as dark as the skies outside his house. Velcro knew something was making her master unhappy, so she laid her head in his lap as he sat on the couch staring out the windows.

After an aimless while, Harvey went into his home office and tried to work, but he just could not seem to focus. Nevertheless, he knew he had a ton of things to do by morning to clear his plate so he could meet Roberta in Tacoma at 7:00 PM. Harvey muttered, "Well, I had better get busy, so I don't miss a chance to see Anna." He found a second wind and finally dug in.

Sometime around midnight, he decided he had all his brain could handle and needed to get to bed. As he was putting his papers in his briefcase, he heard Velcro growling. She ran out of the room toward the front door, jumping up on the windowsill by the double front doors, and started barking with vigor. Harvey had never heard her bark like this, so he knew something was not right. He went to the office window to peek out in the front and saw a car speeding up the driveway and tearing around the corner.

"Velcro, come here girl," commanded Harvey. The dog came running like she knew she had just saved the day.

"Good girl, good girl. You made them go away, didn't you?" Harvey patted her on the head and lavished her with praise for hearing something he didn't hear.

He remembered that he had never called Pete to let him know about the car that had shown up now three times. He grabbed his phone and called the police. He told them what had happened at his home and that he had seen the car two times before. Unfortunately, Pete was not on duty and would not be back until tomorrow. The police wanted to know if they should send a car out to check things out and Harvey told them no. He was sure that whoever they were, they had been scared off for now. He would turn on the alarm and, of course, he had Velcro. They agreed it was probably just some people looking to get in trouble. He asked them to leave a message for Pete and told them it was very important.

Harvey turned off the lights and turned on the house alarm. He got his 9mm Glock pistol out of its safe and checked to see if it was loaded. He grabbed a box of shells and headed to bed.

CHAPTER 9

HARVEY WAS ONE OF TWO LEAD COUNSELS FOR A BANK-ing giant that was facing a class action lawsuit. He had been put on this case due to a similar case that he won in New York a few years earlier. This current case, however, unlike the one in New York, appeared to have teeth. There was solid proof of negligence on the part of the bank, with plenty of evidence, but he was still working to find a way out for his client.

He had several depositions scheduled with participants of the suit at his downtown office in Seattle. Early in the morning, he put Velcro in the car and dropped her off at daycare. He never liked leaving her alone in the house when he had things scheduled down-town since his schedule could change quickly during a day. He never wanted Velcro to be left for that long, especially now with all this 'stuff' going on.

Despite the importance of his case, Harvey was having a hard time keeping focused. His mind kept wandering back to that Friday night, to Anna in the hospital, and, of course, to the thugs almost breaking into his house.

"What the matter with you today, Harvey?" asked Gunner, the other lead attorney, as they were standing in the break room.

"I had a hell of a weekend," Harvey answered. "In fact, it's almost unbelievable. So bizarre that it doesn't seem real. But trust me, I'm not dreaming."

"Why, did you end up spending the weekend in Chicago and getting a little action?" Gunner snickered.

Harvey shook his head. "Not that kind of unbelievable. I caught the last flight out of Chicago and was thankful to be home. But I had no warning that I would get involved in a crime." Harvey saw the look of shocked concern on his friend's face. "Say, do you have a couple of minutes to chat so I can fill you in?"

Gunner, who's actual name is Guthrie, was one of Harvey's closest friends, even trying to set him up with women who were friends of his wife. They had all met in college and formed a strong friendship, but Gunner left New York years before, He had been with the firm for about three years although he said he was still getting his sea legs. Even from a distance, Harvey had been a really big influence on Gunner. The two had built an even stronger relationship since Harvey arrived in Seattle.

Gunner was one of those guys that ran deep, although you never knew it because he was such a cut-up. Gunner had a very rough start growing up in the streets of Chicago. His older brother had been involved in a murder over a drug deal and was murdered in prison for turning 'state's evidence'. His dad was killed by a gunshot fired at him by mistake. Gunner was eight at the time and still struggled with his dad's death every day of his life. He made a commitment to himself the day they buried his dad that he was getting out of this neighborhood never to come back.

Gunner's mom was an addict, so his dad was all he had back then. After the death of his dad, he was put in foster care where, dealing with trauma issues, he acted out and was moved to new foster homes numerous times. At the age of sixteen, Gunner was approached by a gang from his old neighborhood. The day they came to him was the day he decided he wanted a better life.

The rest, as they say, is history. He buckled down, studied hard, finally got out of foster care and worked at several jobs to earn scholarships to go to college. There were times he held down three jobs and still carried a substantial load at school. He was a brilliant guy; math and science were a breeze for him. But he had a deep river of compassion for the law and how it affected kids in foster care. Having stood in court with no control over his life and no one caring what he had to say, he knew firsthand that the entire juvenile system was screwed up so badly it was almost not repairable. He had suffered at the hands of complacent social workers and lousy foster care families who abused him. No matter what he told his so-called advocates, no one believed him. Eventually, he just gave up and took whatever the judge gave him.

When his mom overdosed the second year he was in college, he was left feeling desperately alone. He buried his head in his studies and excelled, ending up at Harvard Law School. He met his wife, Sloan, there and from that point on, his life was pure joy. To pay off his college loans and keep a family intact, he ended up moving into corporate law where the real money was made. He had no other choice.

Gunner never looked back about not going into juvenile law but he still felt the pang of knowing thousands of children were left to fend for themselves. Although sometimes it ate him alive, Gunner was very good at convincing himself he had done the right thing. After all, he was a damn good attorney.

Harvey was always pretty quiet about his own personal life and did not share with a lot people. He was at ease with Gunner, sharing more of himself with him than with anyone, including Cassie. Their stories bonded them together with a strong sense of brotherhood. Maybe it was Gunner's brutal honesty, or the fact that his in-laws were also from the Hamptons that helped bring them together. For whatever reason, the closeness had led Gunner to recommend Harvey as a partner in the firm, another thing for Harvey to be grateful for.

Harvey and Gunner sat down at the table in the break room and waited for the room to clear. Each grabbed a stale, left-over donut from the counter and Harvey unfolded the whole weekend saga.

Gunner listened intently and said, "Dang Harvey, you weren't kidding about a hell of a weekend! I will tell you, as your friend and favorite attorney, you need to get some 'skinny' or something on these guys. Sounds like they are trying to spook you or even come after you for something. That could be pretty serious. And the baby, wow, what a trip! What are you going to do, man? You going to be all right?"

"I'm doing exactly what I need to do, I guess. I'm seeing Anna, the baby, tonight. She was something incredibly special, Gunner. I don't know how to explain it because you know I'm not normally a 'kid' person. I don't know if it was finding the baby in such a horrible situation or what, but she stole my heart. I have never felt so much compassion and love for any kid in my life! I mean you remember that Cassie and I didn't even want kids. Well, I did, but she didn't, but it certainly wasn't one of the main needs in my life. I don't know what the pull is, but I feel like I've got to see this through. I know Anna's safe now, well relatively safe, but I've got to see this through." Harvey paused and took a bite of his cruller. "And then," he continued, "there's Roberta."

"Say what?" squealed Gunner. "Roberta who? So, from the lift I just heard in your voice, I can tell you're not talking about some poorly dressed, oversized, underachieving, coke-bottle-glasses toting social worker, are you? Dude, you're in worse shape than I thought!"

Gunner grimaced and Harvey knew he was remembering some of the social workers he had dealt with. He hadn't liked any of them and Harvey knew he could still recite them all by name complete with a special insult for each. Harvey had heard him do it before.

"Well, yes and no," Harvey calmly replied. "She is sort of a social worker. She's head of Child Protective Services in Pierce and a few other counties. As for poorly dressed or oversized, nope, certainly not. She's not an underachiever with a double master's in social work and child psychology. No glasses either. In fact, she's probably the most sophisticated, beautiful, confident, and knowledgeable woman I've ever met. And stainless-steel smart!" Harvey added with a tiny, crooked smile.

"Well, Harvey Waggoner, bless your little heart. I do believe you're smitten! Can it be that there's finally a woman in your horizon?" Gunner teased, a big grin splitting his face.

"No, no, no, it's nothing like that," Harvey protested. "She's just a very important woman to me right now. She's my ticket to see Anna and keeping up with what's going to happen to her. Don't go jumping to conclusions my friend." Harvey got up to get back to his office.

"Okay, Mr. I-don't-want-to-get-involved-with-any-woman! We'll see," Gunner replied.

Harvey got back to his office to find that his next deposition had to be rescheduled due to illness. He'd thought about calling Officer Pete all day, and this seemed the best opportunity.

He finally got Pete on the phone after a couple of tries and the two chatted a little about their weekends. Harvey began explaining about Anna and how tragic her situation had turned worse. Pete said that he was aware of the details but that the detectives from Tacoma were still on the case. In fact, he was scheduled to meet with them later that afternoon.

Finally, Harvey told Pete about the car and the intruder at the door. "Send me over the pictures you took, and I'll run some plates," Pete instructed.

While they finished up their conversation, Harvey sent over the photo of the car. He really loved the convenience of technology, he thought.

Harvey finished up his work and was lucky enough to be the last car on the ferry to Port Orchard at a reasonable hour. *Good*, he thought. *I can pick up Velcro and grab a burger and then head to Mary Bridge Children's Hospital.* He really loved leaving the office and riding on the water to get home; it was so very peaceful and usually very smooth, so much better than driving on the I-5 with all the traffic. Each time he was on the waterway, he found something new to gaze at on the ride.

Harvey picked up Velcro and a burger for each of them on the way home. Velcro was really excited since she knew there was a burger for her as well. She could hardly sit still in her seat. But as they pulled up to the house, Harvey had an odd sensation that something was terribly wrong.

CHAPTER 10

AS HE DROVE DOWN THE GRAVEL DRIVE, HE COULD see from tramped on flowers that someone had been in the bushes. The eight-foot ladder that had been lying in the grass had been moved. As he got closer, he noticed what appeared to be a dirty handprint on the window. He slowly edged toward the house and noticed the front door was closed. He knew the alarm had not been breached since he would have been notified.

He pulled to a stop at the front door and gave a command to Velcro, "Stay." Velcro stood on her hind legs with her nose pressing against the window, softly growling as she watched Harvey walk along the front of the house.

He was very careful where he stepped, trying not to mess up the footprints that might be a clue. He walked along the side of the house and noticed two deck chairs that were leaning against the house had been dislodged.

He had a sick feeling that those same men must have been there. Possibly they were scared off by the alarm posting, but the video camera hidden on the porch might have gotten an image of them. It was pretty clear they were looking into the house to see how it was laid out.

Harvey whipped his cell phone out to call 9-1-1, just as a black sedan pulled into the driveway, followed by a police car.

By now, Velcro had stopped growling and was outright barking and ready to attack. Harvey opened the car door and said, "It's okay girl. It's okay." He unleashed her and she leapt out of the car to stand at attention by her master as the three men approached. She stayed rigid but continued a low growl until Harvey calmed her down.

"What the heck? I was just going to call you," said Harvey, recognizing Pete and the two Tacoma detectives.

Pete jumped forward and said, "Harvey, we hate to drop by unannounced, but we have something important to tell you."

Harvey waved his arm around behind him. "It looks like those guys I told you about came out to take a closer look at my house," explained Harvey.

He pointed out all the places where the intruders had left their mark. The detective who Harvey remembered was named Robert James looked nervous and said, "We'll call for reinforcements to come out and take some prints and photos if that's okay."

Harvey shrugged. "I'm anxious to hear what you have to tell me, but I'm more interested in stopping these guys that keep showing up on my door."

"Believe me, you're not as anxious as we are, Harvey," said Pete giving him a reassuring smile. "Let's go in and chat for a few."

Harvey looked at his watch since he did not want to be late to meet Roberta. "I've got to get out to the hospital to meet up with Roberta McEniry from CPS. I'm going to try and see Anna and I don't want to miss that opportunity," he explained.

"I think we'll be out of here in plenty of time, but you'd better sit down and listen to what we have to say before you decide if you need to reschedule your appointment," Pete answered curtly.

Harvey sat on the couch with a hundred questions running through his head. Velcro joined him, sensing the atmosphere in the room.

"Robert, why don't you start and explain the situation we've got going on here?" Pete said.

"Mr. Waggoner, there has been new information that has come to our attention in this case," stated Detective James. "We have discovered that the situation you came upon last Friday night was an active crime scene. We haven't put all the pieces of the puzzle together yet, but we do know for sure you must have interrupted something going down involving the blocks of heroin and AK-47 rifles. We are not exactly sure how the woman and child fit in, but we're working on that."

Robert cleared his throat and continued, "It turns out that the car was stolen. The drugs appear to have been part of a shipment from the Mexican cartel along with the guns. Thing is, when a shipment is made by the Mexican cartel, they count every block, every bullet, every gun that is to be delivered. If the numbers don't add up on delivery, then, well, there's hell to pay, often including someone's life.

"The DEA and the FBI have had an eye on this particular runner for the cartel for some time. He had apparently stolen from the cartel thinking that it wouldn't be found out. We figure that he then

60

stole a car and put the drugs in the backseat. We're still not sure how the woman ended up with the car but we knew that our runner had a girlfriend that he'd been seeing for a while. Either the runner was trying to escape from the cartel's clutches, or the girlfriend was. Apparently, they didn't succeed."

The detective shook his head. "Assuming that the dead woman was his girlfriend, it fits in with our information that our guy beating her even while she was pregnant. I guess hegets his jollies by hurting people since he has a rap sheet a mile long for abusive crimes. We are thinking that he stole the car to hide his pilfered drugs until the coast was clear and he could get them moved. We also think he probably beat the woman earlier that day and she took her baby and ran off in the stolen car not knowing the drugs were in the vehicle. You know she was at the local police station asking for help and, as you've already heard, no one took her seriously."

The other detective, Martin Cowell, stepped into the conversation and said, "We believe he found her trying to get away and beat the hell out of her, leaving her unconscious. We believe he must have tried to shut up the baby by slapping her and that is where she got the residue of fentanyl on her person. Keep in mind, sir, that this is all a theory, not something at the moment we can prove. But based on the MO of this particular runner, it's a scenario that fits all the facts."

Cowell then took a deep breath and continued. "This all happened on a road that is not widely used at 2 AM. We think that a couple of guys had come to retrieve the drugs out of the car since we found truck tracks right in front of the parked car. The tracks show signs of a hasty exit. You showed up and probably scared them off. Then you were there until the police arrived shortly thereafter and stayed on the scene for a while. We believe they were watching you the entire time and they may think you either have some knowledge about the drugs and guns, or that you've stolen them yourself."

"We are assuming that they returned after the police had processed the crime scene but by then the car was being towed. Therefore, the only connection that they can get your hands to try to reclaim their contraband is you," Robert said with compassion.

"Are you telling me these guys are after me because they think I've stolen their stuff?" Harvey asked as his voice cracked.

"Yes, or at least that's what we believe at this moment. We're sure they probably got your license plate, or they followed you home," Martin explained. "These are very bad guys, Mr. Waggoner. They are very bad for your health. The DEA has been watching this runner and his partners for some time. We know one thing for sure – these are not just a few rogue guys. They are organized, armed, dangerous, and loaded with money. And they're laser focused on getting heroin, fentanyl, or anything else they can sell illegally across the border. They run it right up the I-5 corridor to Vancouver and on into the rest Canada. This is a precision operation to spread drugs all through North America."

"We don't mean to scare you," Robert cut in. Then he gave a worried smile. "Well, yes, actually, we do. These are professionals and would not hesitate to take anyone out that is in their way. We've arrested several of their people and just know they have the power to get into our system and find these people and have them killed. This specific Mexican cartel group is the second largest deliverer of drugs, prostitutes, and trafficked children in the United States, second only to a group that works from Texas. We estimate this group does mor than a billion dollars a year in business. Billion with a B. Therefore, it's very important that you do exactly as we ask. We believe you are a target because this small-time player screwed the cartel and now, he's in a panic."

Harvey sat in disbelief. He was having a hard time wrapping his head around the fact that his life was in danger, that a drug runner had beaten and killed Anna's mother, and on top of all that had harmed Anna. He did not know whether to cry or to be furious.

Trying to gain his composure, he looked at his watch and knew he was never going to make it to Mary Bridge to see Anna. He needed to call Roberta. He told the visitors his situation and excused himself, going into the kitchen to make his call.

Roberta answered on the first ring. "Hi, Harvey," she said, a little breathlessly, "I was just about to head out to the hospital. I'm looking forward to meeting you there."

"Listen, Roberta, there's been a change in plans. I can't explain now, but I'm not going to make it. I have the detectives back out at my house," he said.

"Is there something new in the case?" asked Roberta.

"Big time, but I'll have to explain later. Please understand that it'd have to be something pretty important to keep me from seeing Anna," Harvey said with sadness.

He could feel Roberta smile on the other end of the line. "Don't worry about it, Harvey," she said. "We'll try this another time. I'm very interested in hearing what's going on in the case. Oh, and I wanted to update you that Anna is not responding very well to the treatment they're giving her. She still hasn't regained consciousness."

"I sure didn't want to hear that," Harvey sighed. "I'll call you when I can. I want to see her, and you, as soon as possible."

CHAPTER 11

ARVEY CAME BACK FROM THE KITCHEN AND JOINED the three police officers again. They talked for another hour or so while the forensic team did their work outside the house. Velcro seemed deeply disturbed by the whole intrusion. She would lay her head on Harvey's lap while the other guys talked, but whenever Harvey said something, her head would pop up and she seemed to listen intently.

"So, what do you want me to do?" Harvey asked. "How can I protect myself against something as immense as the second worst Mexican cartel?" Harvey asked softly. He had to admit, he was scared. He had read about the many Illegal immigrants getting across the borders who engaged in the sex trade, brought in drugs laced with poisons, and all of their other atrocities. He was totally unsure as to where he was heading.

Get a grip on yourself! He thought. *You won't do any good by panicking.* He talked himself down from the horror picture he kept seeing in his mind. He turned his mind to thinking how horrible it must have been for Anna when this animal would rough her up for crying. He traded fear for anger and that gave him strength and resolve.

"Just tell me what to do and let's do this," Harvey said firmly.

Robert said, "We are working with the DEA on this and officially they have the lead. Martin and I, along with Officer Murdock, will put our efforts toward solving the murder. Unfortunately, the case is tied to the Mexican cartel which than makes it too complex for us to tackle alone. Rest assured, though, our main goal is to keep you safe. By the way, the license plate that you gave us was from another stolen car. This new evidence and what we can pull from today's visit hopefully will get us a little closer to the perpetrator's real identity.

"Meanwhile," he continued, "we are going to post someone outside for a while to see if your visitors come back. We recommend that you leave or stay with friends. At the very least, use your security system even while you're at home. And keep your phone with you at all times. Do you have a weapon?"

"A 9 mm Glock, and I'm very proficient," replied Harvey. "I used to go to shooting ranges in New York just to calm down. Also, I've had a bunch of classes in safety and shooting straight."

"Registered?" asked Pete, cocking his eyebrow.

"It's registered and I have a concealed permit."

The agents all got up to leave and Robert reached into his pocket and pulled out a business card. "This is a cell number where you can reach me night or day. You call me if anything, and I mean *anything*, goes down. If you remember something from Friday night, whether an image you might have seen, a smell, anything at all, contact me or

Martin. We're not going to let you face this alone. We're pretty good at our jobs, Mr. Waggoner. Pete is here too so stay in contact with us. If you must go downtown to your office, let us know. We don't know what resources these murderers have available but we're sure that they won't be limited just to the Peninsula."

Harvey finally got them out the door and headed back toward the kitchen. It was then that he remembered he had left the burgers in his car and that they had yet to eat. He went out the front door with Velcro on his heels and retrieved the bag.

As he headed toward the kitchen it occurred to him that he had forgotten to turn on the security system. *This is going to be a pain turning the system on and off all the time*, he thought. Still, it was a small price to pay for staying safe.

• • •

While this was going on, Roberta was sitting in the hospital waiting room with her mind wandering in a hundred directions. The foster mom had gone in to see Anna again and Roberta was just exhausted. She had been running non-stop at work, especially on this case, and she needed to just stop and breathe a little. Anna's case had taken a huge toll on her. Dealing with a child with a murdered mom was not something she fancied, but sadly it was not a new experience. Though her stamina was amazing for a woman in her early forties, this specific case had her going for sure.

She had discovered that the mother's name was Sylvia Brown Taylor, born in Redding, California, where she dropped out of school in her sophomore year. Her father was dead and her mother was in prison. She had been in and out of foster homes most of her teenage life. After her dad died of a heart attack when she was thirteen, her mother took up an old habit of drugs and alcohol and it wasn't long before Sylvia had been sexually abused by her boyfriends and left to care for herself. The CPS got wind of her situation from the school, removed her from the home, and put her in foster care. It had been downhill from there.

As far as Roberta could find out, there was one sibling, a half-sister. However, there was no sign of her anywhere. The state of California had never been able to identify Sylvia's mother's family and her dad was an only child whose parents were dead. But Roberta needed to look under every rock since the state always prefers to put a child, especially one as young as six months old, with a blood relative. Roberta had to admit that sometimes, the state gets blind on relatives. They want a 'blood relative' so badly that they overlook obvious points of danger for the child. She had seen courts send small children to a third cousin who lived in squalor – the cousin accepted because they thought they'd get money. This is where Roberta and her ex-husband parted opinions. Protect the child at all costs. She knew all too well that didn't always apply to every judge or in every courtroom.

The state provides for these ne'er-do-well parents who have abused, neglected, or abandoned their kids in exchange for drugs or alcohol. Attorneys are furnished for each parent. Often warm housing, food, and clothes were given to the failing parents as well. Sometimes the attorneys lose sight of what should be the main objective, the safety of the kids. They get so wrapped up in a win or lose situation that the kids become no more than a footnote. Sometimes they're so convincing that, even if everyone working on the case knows differently, the judge is left without many alternatives. The system has never really been overhauled to focus solely on what is best and safest for the child.

Anna's mother Sylvia was 26 years old at the time of her death and had a record for drug possession and prostitution. Roberta had seen this played over and over a thousand times in her career. Some young, good-looking, naïve girl hooks up with a guy who promises her everything. He moves her out of her comfort zone to a place where there are no friends or family for her to lean on. Then he beats her and pimps her out for money, or worse yet, outright sells her to the highest bidder. Sylvia had been young and very pretty from the pictures she had seen. You couldn't tell that from her beat-up face when she died, but she was definitely a 'looker'. Roberta could see why she would have been perfect bait for some greasy dude. These kinds of people prey on kids that are in foster care since the girls usually who have a poor self-image, no contact with relatives, and become an easy mark for sex traffickers and thugs.

Roberta had been in a situation like this one in her life, but she made it out alive. Her parents divorced when she was just ten and after that her mother went a bit wild and crazy. The official story was that her mom was bi-polar and refused to take her medication. For whatever reason, her mom got caught up in prescription drugs and alcohol, which ultimately ended her relationship with her daughters. Roberta's dad moved in with some young woman, so she and her sister were left alone most of the time. The odd thing about this is that her dad was a pastor. He once had a medium-sized church under his care and apparently, as she discovered years later, he was having numerous sexual affairs with women there.

Roberta didn't believe her mom was really crazy, but that her dad drove her crazy. Their life had been straightforward until her dad left the family. Roberta supposed that her mom and the girls were naïve about the real world. Her dad claimed that he didn't really mess with those women that the people were making things up because the devil was after him for doing such good work. The sad part was that Roberta believed that in the beginning. But as things got out about her father, Roberta's friends started treating her and her sister differently. She just couldn't understand. Finally, all the allegations of sexual misbehavior were confirmed, and her dad was fired.

After her dad left, her mother began bringing home creepy guys. It was like her mother had gone off the rails, acting like a person she didn't know. Roberta and her sister teamed up and became inseparable to protect each other from the horror that was tearing their family apart. Too many times the men her mom brought home would be after Roberta and her sister as well. All of them seemed to use the F-bomb with every other word. Roberta had to do some investigating to even know what it meant and was horrified when she found out. She and her sister had one friend, a boy down the street who was two years older and would teach them about the world at large. He was the only way to get information, since they had no church, no other friends and even the teachers even looked at them funny. They had no place to turn.

One night, one of their mom's boyfriends slipped in their bedroom and raped Roberta and her sister. They tried telling her mother, but she refused to believe it and turned on the girls. men- the man told them that he would kill their parents, their dogs, and their friends if they tried to tell told anyone else. Often, he would hold a knife to Roberta's throat while he raped her sister, and then threaten them that he would come back and slit their throats in the middle of the night if they told. Or he threatened to take them away from school and move them away from everybody they knew. Many nights, he wouldn't rape them but would come into their bedrooms and threaten them with the knife just for the fun of it. Roberta knew that she would remember to her dying day the fear and sickness that came over her as he slid his slimy, grubby hands all over her body.

The passion of those horrible memories was the force driving her to chase down those who just give up on their children as if they were worth nothing. She had turned her life experiences into a finely honed skill set to communicate with kids effectively and compassionately in peril. She had been in situations similar to many of the kids she dealt with daily and she was able to read the invisible signs. The kids sensed her shared experience and often trusted her, a skill that won her admiration from her peers.

• • •

Roberta was jolted from her introspection when Anna's foster mom came into the waiting room where she was sitting. The woman plopped down in the chair next to her and put her head in her hands and cried.

"I know I've only had her a few days, but my heart is breaking for that poor baby girl. I just feel like I need to push for something from these doctors, or do something to help Anna," said the foster mom in despair.

Roberta put her arm around the woman's shoulders and gave her a little hug. "Listen, I've been known to be a pretty demanding woman when it comes to my child's safety and health, but neither of us can do anything at this moment except what we're doing. We can pray and hope for the best," she said warmly.

"Anna is having difficulty breathing and they are taking her in to see if her lung has collapsed. I am just sick over this. I feel so help-less," the foster mom said. "Any word on who killed her mamma?"

"I think you've got your hands full right now taking care of that little girl without worrying about something you have no control over. The police are pretty good at their job and I'm sure they'll find something out soon. You need to stay focused on meeting Anna's needs," Roberta said firmly.

The foster mom got up again, thanking her for the encourage-ment, and returned to Anna's room. Roberta slipped back into her thoughts again.

Roberta recalled when she and her sister were turned over to CPS. They were split up to go to different foster homes. Roberta had grieved deeply to have her sister with her. She knew she was the stron-ger of the two, being the oldest, but the separation proved to be even more crushing than finding out about their dad. Roberta, and her sister Rebecca, were all they had. It was a dark, dark time in her life.

Roberta had spent most of her time away from her sister, being angry at the world, and so she spent a lot of time acting out and get-ting moved to different foster homes. After her seventh move, she realized one day in school that she only had control over what she could do and not what others would do. She made a conscious deci-sion to find a way to be with her sister and she knew that could only be accomplished by letting go of her anger and using her brain. She dug deep and straightened out her life. She had always been smart and now she got great grades in school and stayed out of trouble.

This seventh foster home was different than the others. There was real love there and, from Roberta's point of view, the foster mom really cared. She was attentive, showing up for school events and helping with projects. Roberta felt like part of this family. Roberta was in high school now and had developed a desire to go to college. She didn't know how she would manage it, but she desperately wanted to go. The family changed her perspective on foster care altogether. Roberta had no idea there were homes like this that could really make a difference. One day, as she was pining for her sister, Roberta decided to talk to her foster mom about it. The two sat at the kitchen table and Roberta shared what had happened in her life and the bond that she and Rebecca had for each other. It was almost as if she felt like this woman was the mother she once had in her life.

They talked for a few hours, sharing tears, fears, hugs, and dreams. The foster mom looked at Roberta and said, "How about I talk with the Social worker and see if I can't get Rebecca to live with us?"

CHAPTER 12

SITTING IN THE CHEERY WAITING ROOM AT MARY Bridge Children's Hospital in her daydreams, Roberta caught herself smiling. "Now, that was a turning point in my life, "she said out loud as if she were having a conversation although no one was there.

Roberta realized that her seventh foster mom's gesture was why she had dedicated her life to these thrown-away kids. Babies like Anna and so many others like her need someone with leverage to be on their side. It was a balancing act that she did in almost every case; balancing her convictions with the courts that often failed, her desire to put the child first with what the state mandated regardless of what was best for the child.

When her foster mom worked it out so Rebecca could live with her again, it was magical. Then and there, she knew what her purpose in life would be. She never looked back. She excelled through the rest of High School, earned a scholarship, and graduated from college with high honors. She proceeded to earn a master's degree in social work and then felt compelled to get a master's in child psychology as well, all while working several jobs. She was consistently ranked at the top of her class. With her credentials, she could probably get a higher paying job with better working conditions, but then who would make sure these kids found their way?

Rebecca went on to graduate as well, but she found that perfect person to share her life with, married and eventually had a couple of kids. But Roberta never considered that path, especially not the children. She never quite got over how a perfectly normal Midwestern Christian family could fall apart so horribly. She didn't want to bring children into the world without the guarantees of a strong family to support and nurture them.

She was startled out of her fog by her cell phone. It was Harvey. Somehow, her heart smiled inside. She really thought a lot of this man. Here was someone who didn't have to get involved with the life of a child, but he did. She admired him for taking this case so personally, because he must just be that kind of a guy.

"Good to hear from you Harvey," she greeted him, a little flustered to hear his voice after thinking about him so fervently.

"Same here Roberta," Harvey answered. "How is Anna doing?"

"Not very well, I'm afraid. The doctors think she might have a collapsed lung," Roberta reported. "They're taking x-rays now. She just doesn't seem to be improving. The foster mom is pretty upset."

"I really hate to hear that… I really do," said Harvey warmly. "But I have to tell you, I've had a truck load of crap fall in my lap with all this."

"What do you mean a 'truck load of crap', did they find the guy that beat up Anna's mom?" she asked.

74

"Not yet although they have some leads," he answered. "But that's only part of the story. I really don't want to talk about this over the phone, but things are getting very intense. Can we meet somewhere for a glass of wine or some coffee? Whichever you'd prefer. I could drive into Tacoma to meet you, if you want."

"Well, I live in Gig Harbor, so why don't we meet at Anthony's on the waterfront in downtown Gig Harbor? I haven't had a bite all day and, honestly, this plan sounds really good right now." responded Roberta.

"How about an hour from now, say 7:30 PM?" he asked.

"Perfect, I'll see you there. I'm almost done here. I just need to check with the on-duty charge nurse to file some paperwork."

As she hung up the phone, she felt more lighthearted than she had in weeks. She tried to analyze it, telling herself she was being stupid. That he's just a person involved in this case, and he just wants to catch up on what's happening to Anna. But in her heart, she could not help thinking or maybe hoping that there was something else there.

• • •

Roberta arrived at Anthony's promptly at 7:29pm. She scanned the restaurant but didn't see Harvey. The young hostess standing behind the desk asked if she might be Roberta.

"Why, yes. That's me," she said in surprise.

"Mr. Waggoner wanted me to tell you he's waiting for you downstairs in the bar."

Roberta thanked her, then headed down the stairs. She spotted Harvey rising from his seat in a booth to greet her. She took a deep, cleansing breath. Anthony's Restaurant was one of her favorite places to unwind. The view of the harbor was amazing and the food was always fresh. She was really looking forward to this meeting.

They sat down and Roberta ordered a glass of Chardonnay and Harvey waited for her to scan the menu and decide what to eat. She was hungry, no doubt about that, so she selected one of their specialty salads and sat back to enjoy her evening. Harvey ordered a salad as well because the cold hamburger he had shared with Velcro hadn't done him much good.

"So, tell me," Harvey asked as soon as they settled with their drinks, "how long have you lived in the Harbor? I had no idea you lived out here with the rest of us 'don't-want-to-be-in-the-city' people." He smiled at her over his frosted mug of beer.

"I moved to the Peninsula after I got divorced a long time ago. I need a quiet place to recharge my batteries after my days full of fighting the courts and attorneys, and looking after kids who don't have a clue where they'll end up next."

They continued their talk, getting to know each other a little better until their food arrived. Roberta was so hungry she thought she was going to eat the plate. Harvey could tell that she was anxious and decided not to bring up what he had been through until a more relaxed moment. Instead, they chatted about schools, jobs, and about their lives. Harvey felt comfortable enough to share about his loss of Cassie. Roberta was moved by the tenderness with which he spoke about her. She loved hearing the story about the move to Seattle. She had no idea he lived so far out, although now it made sense why he was on that road the night he rode to Anna's rescue.

Both Roberta and Harvey found it odd that they felt so at ease and just talked as if they'd been friends for years. They were not people who opened up easily, but they were sharing stories without reserve. For two people who had chanced to cross paths barely a week ago, they were now forming a very strong bond with each other.

They stayed at the restaurant much longer than either had anticipated. Harvey had stuff to do for work and Roberta had a mountain of things facing her as well, so they knew they would pay the piper for their time together. But they were both so happy with their new friendship that they did not want to call it a night. Harvey felt like a little schoolboy with his first crush. Roberta had never spent that much time with anyone on purpose.

Harvey walked Roberta to her car and reached over and gave her a peck on the cheek. He said, "I want to thank you for being such an advocate for Anna, and I don't think I've ever met anyone like you. I apologize if I'm being too forward, but I thought we had a good connection tonight over things beyond the murder of Anna's Mom."

"Her name was Sylvia, Sylvia Taylor," Roberta said, plainly. "She was just 26 years old. This is such a tragedy and such a huge loss for Anna. I felt you needed to know Anna's mother's name."

"You're right, I'm sorry for not asking sooner. I got stuck in this frame of mind, and I should have asked," Harvey said quickly.

"I just wanted you to know, for Anna's sake. Now, I've got to go. I've got a lot to do before bedtime. Thank you again for such a wonderful evening." "And I'm thankful that we've connected on a new level as well. And, no," she said.

"No?" questioned Harvey.

"You don't owe me an apology. You were not forward at all. We did have a great conversation tonight. I'm really glad to get to know you better, Harvey," Roberta said with a smile as she got into the front seat of her car.

• • •

Just as he took his exit to his house off Highway 16, Harvey's cell phone rang. It was Officer Pete.

"Pete, what's going on. It's kind of late for you, isn't it?" teased Harvey.

"How far are you from home, Harvey," Pete asked stiffly.

Harvey sensed Pete's tone and became deadly serious. "About ten minutes out. Why?"

"There's been a break-in at your house. You should get here as quickly as you can," Pete stated and quickly hung up the phone.

CHAPTER 13

SPEEDING HOME, HARVEY'S FIRST THOUGHT WAS OF Velcro. He prayed that nothing had happened to her. He thought about calling Pete back to check on her but knew he would be home in a few minutes.

He raced on the nearly empty roads as fast as he could safely drive and finally arrived at his house. Several police cars were parked in his driveway with their lights flashing.

He jumped out of the car, running toward the door shouting, "Velcro, Velcro, come here girl." Just as he entered the doorway, leaping over the couch and a coffee table, Velcro flew into his arms. She was shaking and panting heavily, but Harvey checked her over to make sure she had not been injured.

Only when he knew his dog was okay did he stand up and look around the house. He could hardly believe the amount of damage that the intruders had done. His big, beautiful room had been tossed away. Chairs had been overturned and drawers were spilled out on the floor with their contents strewn everywhere. He peered down the dark hall towards his bedroom just as Pete walked up to him and said, "Harvey, we've had a little problem here."

"No kidding," Harvey proclaimed. "What the hell went on here anyway? How did someone get into my house without me knowing? Who broke in? Why didn't my alarm go off and why wasn't I notified by phone from the alarm company? And, by the way, why are you here?" Harvey said, bullying the questions.

Pete knew he was upset and had every right to be. Harvey had been through it since the incident. His world had been turned upside down. Now he had to deal with this.

"Harvey, I need you to sit down and let the guys have time to finish processing this room," said Pete with as much reasonable calm as he could muster. "And by the way, your dog is really scared. I did the best I could to comfort her, but she wouldn't calm down without you here. We found her hiding under the bed."

Harvey straightened up a few chairs, and then flopped backwards on the couch. Velcro nestled up with her head under his armpit. She couldn't get any closer if she tried. But she finally settled in and began to work through her stress.

Pete explained that they figured the intruders were the guys that had been following him, and that there were probably more than the two that Harvey had seen. They had cut the cable cord to his house, which took the security system offline and then had entered his house through the office window. Pete told Harvey that he'd need to replant the flowers again since they had really messed up the flower beds.

He went on to say that in their investigation of the murder case, they had identified one of the men who they believe was involved with beating up Anna's mother. He had been living with her for a few months and there had been numerous domestic violence calls. Harvey looked at him as though he was in disbelief.

"Numerous calls and you didn't pick him up," Harvey shouted.

Before Pete could respond to Harvey's anger, the front door as it was slowly opened by a tall, thin man that Harvey had never seen. Pete's head instantly turned toward the door and he put his hand on his weapon as he stood up. Velcro began growling and skittered toward the door.

"Whoa there, little buddy," said the stranger, holding his hands in the surrender position, "I'm a friend not an intruder." Pete heard the familiar voice and broke out in a smile. Seeing Pete relax, Harvey called Velcro back and rose to greet the newcomer.

"Chief! Welcome to another crime scene!" Pete said as Sheriff Bloom joined them, sitting down uninvited at the edge of the couch opposite Harvey and Velcro. The dog continued to growl under her breath.

Pete turned to the Sheriff and said, "Chief, this is Harvey Waggoner. Harvey, this is Chief Walter Bloom, Port Orchard's leading Sheriff!" After the two men acknowledged the introduction, Pete continued to address his boss, saying, "You know all about Harvey. He was the one who found that crime scene and helped the little baby. I'm glad you're here but I didn't expect you to come to the crime scene. To what do we owe the honor?"

The Sheriff made himself comfortable on the couch without even acknowledging Harvey's extended hand for a welcome Harvey sat back down and glowered. *That was just rude*, Harvey thought. *Why is this guy, Sheriff or not, coming into a crime scene – my home*

—and just plopping down on the couch without even looking at me. How is this guy so popular around here?

Chief Bloom cast his eyes over the entire house, everywhere but at Harvey himself. "Oh, I just wanted to meet the man that everyone at the station is talking," he said. "Quite the hero you have here, Pete. It's not every day we have a citizen stepping in to help a baby and it's wounded mother."

"She," spat out Harvey. "The baby is a she."

Bloom ignored the hero's interruption as he kept scanning the room. There was something about the Sheriff's manner and tone that annoyed Harvey. Was the Sheriff hinting at something or was he just the arrogant type. Harvey tried to shake the feeling and Pete and the Sheriff began talking. Velcro continued her soft growls. She clearly was not happy with the newcomer either.

If Pete noticed the friction between the two men, he did not acknowledge it. Instead, he continued his briefing, "As I was saying before the Chief arrived, Harvey, the police have their hands tied unless someone files a formal complaint. According to our records, the woman would call us, then the police would show up, but she would never file an official complaint." He sighed under the weight of too much experience. "It's a typical story in abuse cases. Unless the police officers witness a person doing harm to another person, they can't do much else except file a report."

"So, who is the guy? Can't you arrest him on suspicion or something?" asked Harvey.

"The person of interest has not been positively identified as of yet," interjected Chief Bloom. "But don't worry. We're pretty sure we know where to find him," he added darkly.

Pete explained. "We're working on it now, but he's just a piece in the puzzle. It would be nice to get someone higher up in this too."

Sheriff Bloom chose this moment to stand up and nod his head towards the back rooms. "I'm going to have a look around at the damage from the break in. Be right back."

Harvey bristled that the man felt he could just wander around without asking, but then again, this was a crime scene, and he was Pete's boss. He shook away his negative reaction one more time.

When Bloom had left the living room, Harvey sat looked around at the shambles of his once beautiful house. He couldn't believe what had gone on in the last week. The only positive thing out of all this mess was meeting Roberta. He thought about all the emotions that had passed through him during that time, from the unexpected feeling of love and affection for Anna to whatever he was feeling for Roberta. And now this, the shock and fear that the intruders had inflicted. On top of all that, there was his job. For pity's sake, he thought, I have a major case going on and here I am in the middle of all of this!

He was startled out of his thoughts when he heard Pete say, "The punk we're looking for is a hired gun for the Mexican cartel but he's not the small-time runner we initially thought he was. Detective Cowell and the others have turned up information that he may also be an enforcer sent to flush out someone in their system who had betrayed them. We're not sure how the mom fits in the picture any-more, or why the baby was left in the car since they usually leave no witnesses around."

Harvey looked at Pete and said, "Then why me? Why are they after me?"

"You're an unknown to them, which makes you a threat. It's cleaner to take you out of the picture than to leave you alone. You don't understand how these guys work. They're killers. They let nothing stand in the way of their billion-dollar industry. They're not sure what you had to do with what must have been going down, or why you hung around so long. The only thing they do know is that the drugs and weapons were left in the car, and they couldn't get to them. Maybe they've been watching to see if you stashed anything. That would explain this mess at least." He waved his hand around him to take in the wreckage in the house.

"The man we've pegged is named Buford W. Finley, aka Big Brute, aka BB, "Pete continued to explain. "He's no stranger to us or to the Tacoma agents. He's known for his violence and also for messing up women. He enjoys beating them up. There are warrants out for his arrest for everything from sex trafficking, murder, armed robbery, and domestic violence in three states. He's not a slouch. He is an armed, angry, violent killer."

Harvey groaned, "So, what do I do now?"

"Well, to be honest," Pete said, "I would get out of here for now if I were you. But we've already contacted your cable provider and pushed them to get this repaired so that you can have some security if you insist on staying. They'll be out first thing in the morning to get it fixed. The reason things are not worse than they are is because we had an officer watching your house and he saw what they were doing. He called it in but was ordered to stand down."

"Stand down?! Stand down while my house was broken into, and my dog put at risk?"

"He was just one guy with no backup against two killers, Harvey. He did the right thing. He called in his report, and we were on the scene within ten minutes. That's why you still have a house left. I guess they had a lookout because they got away before we could even get here."

As Harvey tried to contain his anger, Sheriff Bloom came back into the room. He waved a quick farewell to Pete and nodded to Harvey and took out the front door. Again, Harvey thought all of the Sheriff's behavior was odd, but reminded himself he had not been a part of a lot of crimes. The crimes he knew were dressed in Armani suits with endless supplies of money, not called 'white collar' crime for nothing. He was totally unfamiliar with these kinds of situations.

Harvey was drowning in the hopeless feeling that this thing would never end. He looked at Pete and said, "I don't have anywhere else to go, and I have Velcro. No way am I leaving without her. Besides, who is going to watch over my place tonight? What if they come back?" he asked.

"Our guess is they won't come back tonight," Pete answered with a sigh. "It's an active crime scene now and they're smart enough to know that. You'd better stay somewhere else, though. Our guys will be working this area for quite a while yet."

"But they could be watching now and follow me wherever I go." Harvey said.

"Well, yeah, that's true," Pete replied. "I'll tell you frankly, Harvey, this has now become a much bigger case than our little city has ever seen. Between the drugs and the murder and the fact that it now crosses state lines, the FBI is getting involved as well. Big Brute is on the FBI wanted list already and they've been scoping out his ties to the cartel. But remember, we don't know if they're after you. They may figure out that you have nothing to do with anything and leave you alone. We just don't have enough information right now. Give us a day or two to sort this out once the FBI arrives here in Tacoma. Till then, we'll do our best to keep you safe. But you had a right to know what you're dealing with, especially now that they've purposely invaded your home."

As Officer Pete went back to work with his squad, Harvey gave Velcro a hug and then picked up his phone. It was already past 11:30 PM but Harvey decided to call Gunner and give him a heads up that he probably would need to work alone tomorrow. Harvey would do everything he could remotely, but he did not want to be too far away from his house. Thankfully, he knew Gunner could handle the two people on the interview schedule.

Gunner was blown away by the new twist on all the things that had happened. He joked that Harvey had brought a big, black cloud back with him from Chicago. Gunner invited him to bring Velcro and stay at their house, but Harvey declined since he didn't want to drive all the way to Mercer Island. Also, Gunner had kids and Harvey did not want to risk getting them involved in any way. The less Gunner knew about any of this, the better. Gunner would not be put off so easily and insisted on making a call or two back to some old friends on the East Coast who were inside the FBI to see if he could find anything out that would help Harvey.

After his conversation, Harvey put some food in Velcro's bowl which she inhaled. She went to be let out, but when Harvey opened the outside door, she huddled back and shook a little.

"Okay, girl," said Harvey. "I get it, you were here when the bad guys broke in and you're still edgy. So am I, to be honest. Here, let me go with you."

As Velcro did her business, Harvey stood in deep thought trying to figure out what he was going to do. Where could he go? He thought about a motel – there was a Comfort Inn just down the road – but he was not sure they allowed dogs.

Just as Velcro came running back, Harvey's phone rang. He looked down and saw that it was Roberta. He thought how odd it was that she would call this late at night, especially since they had just left each other's company. He smiled for the first time since he had arrived home, thinking, *she likes me.*

"Hey, am I ever glad you called," he answered. "You'll never believe what's going on here."

"Harvey, where are you, what are you doing?" Harvey could tell by her strained voice that something serious was wrong.

"Home, standing outside on the patio," he answered, suddenly serious. "What's wrong? Is there news about Anna?"," he said.

"Oh Harvey, I have terrible news. I don't know how to tell you this, but Anna's dead."

CHAPTER 14

HARVEY STOOD AS IF HE HAD BEEN SHOT. AN ALL-TOO-familiar feeling of grief buried his spirit. He felt the same grief and helplessness as when Cassie died. He somehow made his way back into the kitchen with Velcro on his heels and crumpled into a chair. Tears streamed down his face. He felt as if someone had cut his heart out.

"What… what happened?" he sputtered through his tears.

Roberta could sense how broken Harvey was at the news. She tried to answer as gently and firmly as she could. "It seems there was just too much fentanyl that had soaked into her blood stream. Her little body fought as hard as it could, but she just stopped breathing."

She was met by deep silence. She let him take the news in for as long as she dared. Finally, when it seemed as if she would never get a response, she said in a gentle tone, "Harvey, say something. You're worrying me. I'm so sorry to be the one to tell you this, but I also felt you would want to know."

"You can't possibly…" Harvey tried to speak but was too choked up to finish the sentence.

"Yes Harvey," Roberta replied, giving him time to pull it together. "I do understand. I know too well how some people who rescue a child feel kinship and compassion for the little one. It's okay to feel that. And to be overwhelmed by the senselessness of Anna's death."

Harvey slowly pulled himself back from the shock. *After all*, he scolded himself, *you've trained your whole career not to show emotions or feelings. That's the role of a defending attorney: when things aren't going your way, you play like everything is coming up roses. Never let them see you sweat.*

Roberta held her silence silent for what seemed like a long time. She was deeply concerned about his grief and hurt, but it validated her sense that his compassion and kindness were real. I an odd way it drew her closer to him.

Harvey was deciding if he should tell Roberta about the latest events. After all, it wasn't her problem anymore. Her case was over now, with Anna gone. After thinking it through, he knew that Roberta would want to know everything. He decided he respected and liked her enough that he needed to be honest.

"Roberta, you know I'm heartbroken," he said choking back a sob. "As I said, things have become crazy here for me. I was just getting some things together to go find a motel room. Some things have happened since we were together tonight, and I have to get out of the house. Well, they actually began right after I met you and Anna. I haven't shared them for a whole bunch of reasons, but now with Anna gone…" He choked up again. "Oh, Anna! Sweet, poor little Anna," he said almost in a whisper.

"Harvey, forget about a motel. You know I live right here in Gig Harbor. I have three extra bedrooms. You can come and stay here tonight and work out whatever you need to tomorrow. Besides, I don't want you to be alone tonight. Honestly, I don't want to be alone either. Would you come over and at least stay the night? I'll just have to trust that you're not a serial killer," she laughed, trying to ease the mood.

"That's a great offer, but it's not just me. I have a dog, Velcro."

"The more the merrier. Bring him on over. I'm an animal lover too, you know," she replied with a lift in her voice.

"Okay, first of all Velcro is a she, and she's just about the best-behaved dog you'll ever see," said Harvey, sounding a little brighter. "Well, all right then, if you're certain. I could use the company too."

"it's settled then," said Roberta. "Come over whenever you're ready. I keep late hours anyway."

Harvey got the address, and they finished their conversation. As he disconnected, Harvey realized that had it not been for Roberta he would probably never have found out what had happened to Anna. As sad as he was, he was suddenly overwhelmed with gratitude that he had met her that awful Friday night.

Pete and his colleagues were still working in the house, and he had noticed Harvey crying. Concerned as he was, Pete had kept his distance until he felt the time was right to ask what was wrong. After all, he thought, this guy deserves a medal for all the crap he was going through. If it were him, he would be screaming and crying out loud like a baby!

Harvey headed to his room to pack up a few things for his stay with Roberta. As he was walking back to his room, Pete caught up with him to talk. "Is everything okay?" Pete asked sincerely.

"No, not at all, Pete." Harvey turned to square off with the police officer. Pete saw the anger and grief that was overwhelming the man and took an involuntary step or two back. "Anna died tonight," Harvey spat out, venting his emotion. "That little asshole was responsible for Anna's death as well. Now you've got two murders to solve."

Pete was in shock, too. "Harvey, I'm so sorry. I know she was a special little baby girl to you. I could tell even during all the craziness that you had bonded. We'll investigate her murder with every effort we can give."

Harvey filled him in on everything new that he had learned. He then informed Pete that he was going to clear out of the house for the night and that he would be back in the morning sometime.

Pete assured him there would be a police car out front of the house for the remainder of the night. At the very least, if the perps came back there would be someone there to call it in immediately. He reassured Harvey that he would personally lock up the house before he left. He went to inform the rest of the team about Anna, knowing it was going to be hard for him. After all, he had been there that night, too.

Pete threw a few things in a bag and got Velcro's favorite pillow, a blanket and a toy. He went to the kitchen and put some dog food and some treats into a canister and threw it in his bag.

As Pete got in his car and keyed Roberta's address into his GPS, he got a little panicky. What in the world was he doing anyway? He didn't really know this woman and now he was staying at her house.

But the image of Anna passed through his mind, and he thought, *what am I worrying about? I've seen this woman in action during the best and worst of circumstances. She is already a dear friend that is experiencing pain just as I am.* The thoughts helped calm him down.

He arrived at her house and realized that it looked just like Roberta: beautiful, warm, and regal looking. Everything about the façade looked completely in order. It was one of the most beautiful places he had seen. Even though they both lived on the Peninsula, Gig Harbor had a different feeling from where his home was located. He decided that he should drive around the area more to see the full range that the Peninsula had to offer.

Before he could even get out of the car, the front door opened and Roberta stood in the double doors, greeting them with a big smile. Velcro jumped right out of the car and ran up to Roberta. Their host knelt to pat and gave Velcro some love.

Harvey thought how Velcro usually did not run to people. The dog looked back at him and waited for a command but seemed completely at ease with her new friend.

Roberta waved her hand. "Come on in, guys! Make yourself at home. You too, Velcro. I've put a bowl of water for you in the kitchen."

Harvey was touched by Roberta's attention. Here was this 'sort of stranger coming into her house at midnight with his dog and she was welcoming them with open arms. *This is the stuff good books are made of*, he thought.

Roberta showed him to a bedroom in the west wing of the house where Harvey placed his bag. Velcro jumped on the bed, so excited she could barely contain herself. Harvey tried to get her off the bed, apologizing for her behavior.

"Listen, Harvey," Roberta said. "There is nothing off limits for Velcro. When I was married, we had a sweet little boxer that I adored, but my ex got him in the divorce. I've never had the heart to replace him with another dog. So, Velcro is more than welcome anywhere to go anywhere she chooses, including the bed. Okay girl?" She bent down and was rewarded for her kindness with a frantic tail wag and a lick on the nose.

"That's terrible that you lost your dog. So incredibly sad. I don't know what I'd do without Velcro, and I've only had her for a little while. She and I are like butter and bread." He grunted. "I never could stand the thought of being a divorce lawyer and coming up with cruel settlements like that."

She nodded and gave a sad smile and a shrug. "Let's go in the living room and we can have a glass of wine or something," she said, leading the way.

Harvey was even more impressed with the inside than the outside of the house. It was amazing, tastefully decorated, and it seemed massive to him. It was a single level structure with a wing of bedrooms on each end. There was a huge family room, a dining room, and even a room with a pool table and a big screen TV. Like his house, Roberta's did not sit right on the shores of the Sound but had an unobstructed view down to the water. That was where any similarity ended. Roberta's house was like a huge southern mansion, while his was just a small, comfortable house with a killer view. *Oh well*, he thought to himself, *it's just a house. Tonight, we've lost a life.* He thought about Anna again and was clouded once more with grief.

Velcro found her way around the house, sniffing everything on her way. She even found the doggie door from the kitchen, a remnant of the former dog of the house. Velcro went to the doggie door and sat down, whining a little.

Roberta jumped up from the couch and said, "I think Velcro wants to go out. Is that okay with you, Harvey? I have a fenced back yard so she can't go anywhere."

Harvey shrugged and got up himself. He walked in through the kitchen door and said, "Okay girl." Before he could reach her, Velcro jumped right through the doggie door.

"Oh," Harvey said, "I guess I didn't have to get up." Laughing, he returned to the couch. Velcro came back through the portal after she had finished exploring and using her newfound environment.

The two humans stayed up until well past three talking about Anna and Harvey's latest news. He told her all about the break in and how badly he seemed to be mixed up with the Mexican cartel. Roberta said that she had been in social work all her adult career and never had anything quite like this. She was very concerned for Harvey's safety, having learned in her position as head of the department and working with law enforcement just how bad the Mexican cartel was and all they had brought into the city. She frequently received alarming information from the DEA, FBI, and local police about the influx of drugs, prostitution, and human trafficking that was coming up the I-5 corridor and she knew all too well that these people preyed on children in foster care. She also knew that the authorities suspected that there was someone local who was assisting the cartel in their crimes, but she held this fact back, not wanting to alarm her friend too badly.

Harvey found that he was able to tell Roberta everything, as if their conversation had just extended from dinner. Both were relaxed, at ease, and enjoying each other's company. They both wept for a while over Anna's loss, at which point Velcro walked across the couch and sat in Roberta's lap. Harvey was amazed; she had never wanted to sit anywhere but with him.

• • •

Despite the late night, both Roberta and Harvey were up and dressed by seven that morning. When Harvey got to the kitchen, Roberta was already there, coffee brewing and English muffins in the toaster.

"Good morning," Harvey said as he walked into the kitchen. "Before you say anything, please let me thank you for putting Velcro and me up last night and especially for the conversation. I don't think I could have made it alone last night. Knowing you and I had Anna in common really helped me through all this. Thank you from the bottom of my heart." He took her hand and, after making sure it was alright, drew her into a hug.

Roberta was pleased and surprised at this show of affection and hugged him back. Even though the circumstances were terrible, she had had a great time with him. Roberta was always one for making the worst of circumstances tolerable, a skill she had learned from all the foster children she had worked with over the years. She was always quick to give credit to the kids because they were her teachers. She learned from them every day.

"Harvey, I needed you to be here last night, too. You have no idea how much I appreciate you staying with me. My job is never what you would call 'ordinary', but a double murder is way out of my comfort zone."

Roberta was about to say something more when her cell phone rang. She excused herself and stepped a few paces away to take the call.

Harvey was retrieving the muffins from the toaster when he heard her shout into the phone. "What the hell are you telling me? I can't believe this!

CHAPTER 15

EVEN THOUGH HE KNEW THE ANGER WAS NOT DIRECTED at him, Harvey froze like a child caught with his hands in the cookie jar. Roberta hung up the phone and stared out the window, obviously fuming. After a few more seconds had passed, Harvey said quietly, "Roberta is everything all right? Is it something to do with Anna? Can I help?"

His voice seemed to break her trance. She spun around. "I'm so sorry, Harvey," she said. "This is about another case altogether. It's gone totally out of control, and I need to get to the office immediately to see if I can fix it." She began packing her things from the kitchen table.

"If anyone can get it back on track, Roberta, it's you. Is there anything I can do?" he asked cautiously, sensing she was at the edge of a cliff with all of this going on and worried that he had invaded her space.

She was grabbing her coat and making for the door, but she looked back and gave him a warm smile. "No, Harvey thanks, but this one is all mine. I'm sorry to run out like this; I really am. Maybe we can talk about it tonight."

She seemed to make a decision and then turned to face Harvey directly. "I don't want you to leave," she pleaded. "You can stay here all day if you need to. There's a spare key in the drawer under the toaster. Come and go as you please. Please don't think that my leaving you is anything other than another emergency in my crazy world."

She stepped back towards him. "I'll call you this afternoon and we can get together tonight. I mean if you want to. I'm not trying to horn in on your day and I know you have work too. I just…" With a small frantic yell, she suddenly walked over to him, grabbed and kissed him. They shared a long and passionate embrace. Harvey's mind pinged like a slot machine as he tried to figure out this new development. At the same time, he loved every minute.

"Well, if you put it like that, I think I'll just hang around for a while and wait for your call," he said, smiling. She smiled back then rushed out the door.

Harvey stood in total shock, wondering what had just happened. He had not felt a leap in his spirit like this since he and Cassie started dating. Although he hadn't been shy about dating since Cassie had gone, he never had a strong connection with anyone. Well, not like this. This lady was different, very different.

When his heart and brain had stopped racing, Harvey called to check in at his office and to get Gunner up to speed. He had a mountain of work to do, so he needed to go home to get some paperwork and his laptop. He grabbed the spare key, then loaded Velcro into the car.

When Harvey pulled up at this house the internet provider repairmen were working on his house. The lone policeman assigned to watch the place jumped out of his car and met him before he walked in the door, showing his Port Orchard PD badge and introducing himself as Dave.

The two had a short conversation and Dave told him the police crew hadn't been gone very long. It had been a long night, but they felt they got a lot of information that could be utilized by the DEA and the FBI.

As Harvey put his hand on the door to go in, Dave said, "Mr. Waggoner, the guys feel really bad about what happened to the little girl you found. They took extra time this morning getting your place back in order. I thought you'd want to know that."

"No kidding? Was that Pete's idea?" Harvey asked.

"Yes sir, it was. Pete is a good guy, and he feels like you got stuck in a war that's not yours to fight."

"Well, the way I look at it, Dave, is that it *is* my war," Harvey said, glancing up at the cable workers. I didn't have to stop that night. But once I did, it became my responsibility to help bring these people to justice and to keep my community and my dog safe."

As he entered the house, he noted that the officers had placed all the furniture upright and had collected the papers from the floor and put them on the table. They had swept and cleaned the office and hallway as well and had even secured a piece of plywood over the window.

Harvey almost cried again thinking about how Pete had done all this for him, knowing this was probably not routine for anyone else's crime scene. He knew that he and Pete had become friends through all this mess, and he was grateful for the friendship.

The telecom guy came in and reported more unwelcome news. "Mr. Waggoner, I'm sorry, but there's no way we can repair this today. They did a lot of damage to the wires and it's going to take a couple of days at least to get this back online."

"If you can't, you can't, but please do all that you can! I have a lot at risk here," Harvey pleaded.

Velcro had already made her way to the couch as Harvey looked around his beautiful room. At least all the sectional couch pieces were upright this time, but the place still felt broken. He stood there for a long while staring out the windows at the Sound and reviewing all the things that had occurred in the last few days. As he tried to make sense of it all, Roberta's face popped up in his thoughts. *Well,* he thought with a resigned sigh, *here we go. I'm all in this time and I'm going to try and not screw it up.*

With no internet for the foreseeable future and with Roberta's beautiful face and kind offer in his mind, he decided to head back to her house to work. He grabbed a briefcase full of papers and filings that needed to be done then called his assistant to review what was coming up so he'd know where to focus his efforts.

He went to the bedroom and gathered up some more items for another night's stay and then went to the kitchen to gather food and treats for Velcro. He decided to stop by the grocery store on the way back and pick up something to fix for dinner. He'd also pick up a nice bottle of wine. *I wonder if she likes red or white,* he thought. *Oh, what the heck, I'll buy a couple of both.*

"Come on Velcro, let's go," he shouted, heading for the front door.

• • •

Roberta arrived at her office and went into gear. She gave one wistful thought to the fond goodbye that she and Harvey had shared, but then she focused on the case that had interrupted them.

She was still shaking her head in disbelief at the sour turn that the case had taken, but then again, she had seen too many similar cases go wrong to be surprised. That was the power of experience.

She had been on this particular case for almost seven years. Usually, the court has a timeline of under two years for closing out cases, but this one was a nightmare. Anything that could go wrong did, repeatedly. The mother never engaged but she kept putting hope out for her son who adored her, regardless of her shortcomings. Mom knew how to play the system and had won so far. The one who had really lost was the young boy.

Today, he'd taken a gun to school and threatened to shoot people. *How many times have we seen that play out on television in the past decade*? Roberta thought, while cursing the circumstances that had allowed it to happen. This 12-year-old had a past that might have predicted that he would act out one day. In fact, she had expected some sort of craziness from him for the past couple of years as she watched the tragicomedy play out.

Kyle had been abandoned and abused so many times by everyone that he considered family. Now he was sitting in a jail cell accused, *allegedly*, of carrying a loaded weapon to school, after he had posted that he was going to kill someone, he didn't care who. Things looked exceptionally bleak for any future this child has left.

Roberta remembered when he came into care the first time, and then the second time and so many others. His mom was a complete addict and sold her soul for the next hit. She had started dropping Kyle off at the mall when he was just five, telling him not to move until she returned. She had no babysitter except her own mother who was an addict too, and mentally unstable to boot. More times than not, the grandmother would pick him up because Mom just couldn't make it back. Then one time no one showed up for him. Enter the Child Protective Services.

When the grandmother was located, she claimed that Kyle's mother had never called, so the state allowed her to take the child. A case had been officially filed, so Kyle would require oversight from the CPS. But the court felt that this child was with family and therefore he was safe. Roberta remembered thinking, who, in their right mind, would leave a five-year-old child at the mall and expect him to sit there for hours? No food, no water, absolutely nothing. Where were the mall cops? Why didn't they see a child alone and check out what was going on? She relived all the frustration she had felt from the beginning, the sense of everyone dropping the ball. She was getting mad all over again.

This child continued to stay at his grandmother's because his mom was out drinking and partying all the time. Meanwhile. The grandmother was doing her fair share of partying as well. She simply disregarded the fact that there was a small child living with her.

The social worker had reported deplorable living conditions and numerous strange men in the house. So did the CASA on this case. The grandmother would put Kyle in front of the TV and tell him not to pay any mind to what was going on while she had many boyfriends spending the night, sometimes several at a time. The grandmother, like the mom, was addicted to heroin and meth.

They could never catch grandmother in the act because Kyle acted as their look-out. All Kyle wanted was his mom. So, he would patiently wait until she would come and rescue him. After all, she had told him on the phone she would be there, but she never made it back.

Kyle had already been expelled from the Tacoma Public Schools because of sexual advances he made on a preschooler classmate. He apparently went into the stall with another little boy and tried to stick his little penis up that child's butt. The victim was so upset he peed all over both of his shoes.

Kyle had also been warned multiple times about putting his hands up the skirts or down the pants of little girls in his classroom. Finally, the school said enough is enough, and removed him from school entirely. Roberta knew that five-year-olds don't know how to do that kind of thing unless they see it or they are taught. She knew it had to be coming from the home environment. In response, CPS began drop-in surprise visits.

On the first unannounced visit by the social worker, she found the little boy watching pornography with the grandmother's boyfriend. The boyfriend was masturbating, showing the five-year-old how to make 'whoopee'. When she walked into the room, the man slipped his penis back in his pants, leaving the young child glued to the television playing with himself.

The social worker made excuses about having left something in her car, then immediately followed protocol by calling CPS who notified the police. The social worker's supervisor and the police arrived at about the same time, but by then, the grandmother and boyfriend knew they had been caught again and were able to get their stories straight.

When they separated Kyle from the adults, though, the young boy's story was totally different. He even showed police and the social worker how to access porn and make 'whoopee'. He said his grandmother told him it would make him special for his mommy.

The courts placed him in a foster home and Roberta recalled how sad he was. He kept saying that his mother was coming back and she would not be able to find him. Over the next few years, between running away or hitting and messing with other children in the household, he went through several foster homes. People would not tolerate his language, his aggressive sexual actions, or the newer behavior of attacking family pets. The homes turned him away, which made it even harder on a boy in distress.

Roberta remembered one meeting with Kyle where she asked him about his dad. He had said, "Dad told me he didn't want me because he was too busy, but that he loved me anyway." Roberta went after the father to get him to assume some responsibility. The dad was living with his parents and several other siblings. The paternal grandparents finally agreed to take Kyle in and assume responsibility for getting him to the many services he needed, such as counseling. Everyone hoped this would be the final stop for Kyle.

Kyle was ready for first grade, but Roberta had a difficult time getting the school to allow him to attend. They finally agreed after special efforts were put in place which would focus on the boy so that the other children would be safe. Roberta was thankful, as she knew how important getting back to a regular routine under supervision would be to this child. She felt like she had won the lottery.

Unfortunately, Kyle's good streak did not last long before he began doing some of the same things again, this time more aggressively.

As it turned out, the paternal grandparents were not all that stable themselves even though they were clean of drugs and alcohol. They were also not taking him to doctor, dentist or counseling appointments. They always had an excuse. Then, as the result of an innocent but truthful conversation that the social worker had with Kyle one day in the car, CPS began putting the pieces of the puzzle together. As it turns out, the grandparents were physically abusing him as well, even encouraging him to have sex with their dog as well as other physical infractions. It was just too much to imagine for this poor child. Once more, they had to remove him from his family.

Returning to the foster system, he went through eight homes in two weeks. After that, case workers were unable to find anyone willing to foster him, so he was removed from school and slept on the couch in the DSHS visitation room.

Finally, after the social worker and Roberta had scoured every blood relative that could be found, they turned up a second cousin of his mother. She herself was a recovering addict but had made good use of her time during recovery and got her master's in social work. She was single and had a couple of renters living in her big house on a lot of property.

Devastated by the horror this child had been through, agreed to take Kyle in. She felt she was qualified to deal with a child who had been through this high level of abuse and who had been betrayed by his parents and both sets of grandparents. Unfortunately, the situation only lasted for about two months before she could no longer manage him. CPS had to come out and pick him up yet again.

Back again in the system, he went from foster home to foster home until the right one finally came along. The family was perfect for Kyle – they understood the kind of abuse Kyle had suffered since they had already been foster parents to some seriously troubled young people. It took a while for him to settle, but he did fine and got good grades in school, Unfortunately, he was always just a little outside the other kids at school.

Now he was sitting in jail for threatening to murder someone for reasons he could not explain. Roberta bowed her head, recalling what this boy had already been through his entire life, and understanding what he was now facing. The mental piece alone could have a lasting effect on his young life. A tear rolled down her cheek as her heart was broken for this young child who had to take on this ugly, crazy world totally alone. She understood that. She understood it well.

Wrapped up in her sorrow, she was shaken by the ring of her cell phone. She looked at who was calling, then hesitated because she was just not together. It rang again and she muted the ring, not taking the call.

CHAPTER 16

HARVEY WAS PULLING OUT OF THE GROCERY STORE when he noticed two men staring at him from a car. Was he being paranoid or could there possibly be someone following him? *Well*, he thought, *I'm not leading them to Roberta's.* He put his phone in its holder and gave the command to call Officer Pete. As he pulled out of his parking spot, he noticed the car started its engine as well and followed in his direction.

Let's go for a ride, he thought Just as Pete answered his phone. Harvey told him what was going on and that he was being followed.

He heard Pete pull in a deep breath of air, then let it out in an exasperated sigh. "Harvey, let's not do anything stupid. You need to follow my instructions exactly. Are we clear?"

"Yes, I have no desire to take these guys on," Harvey answered. I just don't want them following me."

"Here's what you're going to do." Pete explained. "Head north and use the main roads to get to your house. Take your time. I'll have a team assembled there by the time you arrive and hopefully we can get an up-close and personal look at these two. So far, they haven't broken any laws that we can prove, so I can't arrest them for just following you. But we might be able to get more on them if we make contact. What make and color of car are they driving now?"

While Harvey described the car and what he could see of the riders, he could hear Pete getting into his squad car. "Okay, got it," said Pete. "Now I'm going to put the phone down and radio for some back-up, but don't hang up. Keep talking to me. I want to know every move they make."

Harvey's stomach flipped a bit as thought about what was going on. It was not the most comfortable thing to be playing cat and mouse with dangerous criminals.

Every few minutes, Pete would ask, "Are you still there?" Harvey would respond with a "yeah' or a grunt, but just kept driving on the main roads to get to his house. The closer he got home the more nervous he got.

As he approached his turnoff, Pete told him to pull into the house like normal and go to the front door. Harvey remembered that the cable people might still be there, but Pete told him not to worry about that, just do as he was instructed.

When he rounded the corner to his house, Harvey saw a car planted close to the scrubs. There were two people inside the car who ducked as he drove past them.

Harvey reported this new car to Pete. He was again told to stick to the plan. Just pull into the house, get out of the car, and go inside.

Harvey's stomach was turned fully inside out now. His mind was screaming "Help!" but he knew had to do this. These guys could be the ones that killed Anna and her mother. With this thought, he regained his strength and resolve. He parked the car and even strutted into the house.

As he was heading in, he looked around to see if he could glimpse anyone other than the thugs who were following him. He spotted a man with a police vest and a gun who was squatting inside the shrubs that lined the property. He suddenly felt a little safer.

Harvey went into the house, locking the front door but not bolting it, just as he had been instructed. He went up to the picture window and peeked outside. He could see three other police officers in vests moving quickly around the side of the house.

Pete had told him to sit in the kitchen and not do anything. Harvey texted back to confirm where he would be sitting and was told to keep radio silence from that point on. Harvey went to the kitchen to grab a cup of coffee from the Keurig, glancing out the window again. The police vests were no longer in sight. He began to panic a little although he knew that they must still be there.

As his coffee finished brewing, Harvey tried to sit and relax, but he felt like a sitting duck waiting for a hunter to shoot. He wished he had brought Velcro with him from Roberta's. She would let him know if anyone was coming in.

The unidentified car pulled quietly into the driveway, parking a couple of car lengths from Harvey's SUV. It was parked away from the front windows so it could not be spotted from the house.

The two thugs got out of their car and slinked to the office window where they had broken in before. They carried a pry bar and wire, more than ready to tackle the plywood that spanned the broken glass. When they were in place on top of the smashed flowerbed,

One of the perps nodded, put five fingers up as a signal, and slid out of the bushes to make his way around the house to the back entrance. He disappeared as the one in front looked at his watch.

The minutes in the house passed like hours. Harvey's anxiety was building again. He trusted Pete, he thought, *but dang, this was hard to do*. What if the bad guys came in blazing?

Suddenly, his phone buzzed, and he nearly wet himself at the sound. He saw that it was Roberta calling but he could not get her involved. He pushed the ignore button, now feeling totally alone and uncertain.

The next second, he heard the crackle of the back door's lock being messed with. His heart raced, he broke out in sweat, and he wished he had his gun with him.

As casually as he could, he turned around in the kitchen chair and saw a man waving a gun at him and telling him to open the door. Harvey thought that if he could just live through this, his security system had him on camera.

The gunman kept yelling at him louder and louder, but Harvey was frozen in place and would not move. He remembered that Pete had told him to sit and not move no matter what. He had no idea how hard that little instruction was going to be to follow. By now, the gunman was in a frenzy of anger, flecks of spittle falling over his grizzled chin. He finally took his gun and blew off the doorknob.

As he walked the gun pointed at Harvey's head, there was a flash of a police vest right from behind him. About the same time, the front door flew open and the other gunman rushed in. In no time, police officers and agents in FBI vests poured into the house, grabbing both gunman and throwing them to the floor. To Harvey the movement looked like a choreographed dance. He was still rooted to the spot, unsure of the reality of what he had witnessed.

Everywhere Harvey looked, the house was full of vests, guns, and radio chatter. At last, Pete flew through the front door calling Harvey's name. Pete found him still frozen at the kitchen table.

"Good job, Harvey!" Pete shouted over the clamor of agents securing the crime scene. "You followed your instructions perfectly. Now we have these two for breaking and entering and armed robbery. I'm sure we'll come up with a bunch of other stuff as well. Their car is stolen and there are weapons in the truck along with a small box of fentanyl.

"We've caught our little fish," Pete said with pride. "so Now, I'm sure they'll lead us to the connection we need. Harvey, you were awesome! If you ever want to go into police work, you will be a natural!" said Pete with pride.

Harvey had not moved other than turning his head. He accepted a handshake and congratulations from the FBI lead and then watched motionless as the agent gave the stand down order. All the officers headed to the door.

Harvey, still speechless, looked at Pete with eyes full of relief and gratitude. "Now we can get down to business," said the police detective. He took a seat at the table and began rolling out how they planned to capture Anna's killers.

As they made their plans, Sheriff Bloom appeared at the door as if been there for the entire event. As before, he ignored Harvey and turned directly to his subordinate.

"Looks like we have another situation here, Pete," he said with just the right note of professional concern. "Can you give me a quick run down?"

"You bet Chief, but let's step outside a minute", Pete offered, a little surprised to see his boss at the crime scene yet again. "Harvey needs to catch his breath for a few minutes anyway."

Pete and Sheriff Bloom walked slowly out the front door. Harvey had that feeling in the pit of his stomach again. *Something was not right here*, he thought. He quickly justified everything he was feeling to his shock over the attack piled so closely on top of the loss of an innocent child's life.

CHAPTER 17

P ETE STRONGLY SUGGESTED TO HARVEY THAT HE should stay gone for a few more nights until they figured out where they were in this case and made sure there were no other bad actors in the neighborhood. He confided that it was hard for him to give up the lead to the FBI now, since he had had these guys in his sights for some time now. At least they were finally able to charge them with a crime now. And this crime had teeth.

"So this case turns out to be bigger than we even imagined," explained the police officer. "It looks like there are all kinds of import-ant people whom this might touch – politicians, financial people, who knows who else. I only know it's been going on for years. The FBI claims that they almost have all the pieces to bring this section of the cartel down to its knees. I guess they're afraid that if they let even a small piece of this go, the whole thing can unravel. Still, it would be nice if our department could get some closure."

He reached for Harvey's coffee and took a big swig, looking a little disappointed that it was not something stronger in the glass. "You probably shouldn't hear all this, but I'm telling you as your friend, Harvey. You're not out of danger yet. We have no idea why they would be putting the squeeze on you. Maybe they think you have information about where the contraband has disappeared to, or maybe they think you work with the feds. Possibly they don't know that Anna's mom died and think you might be hiding her. There are a dozen possibilities. Whatever the reason, you need to keep alert until the FBI has this thing sewn up."

Harvey held his head in his hand, overwhelmed by the hundreds of thoughts and possibilities of how his life had been changed. Then it hit him; he had to get back control of his own life. He knew he could be brave. Heck, he had not even flinched when the gunman had aimed at him a short time ago. Besides, he was pretty good with a gun himself, and knew he would never hesitate to use one if some was trying to kill or hurt him or someone he loved. He knew he would even kill if he had to. He felt the tension relaxing and his body began to unwind.

He and Pete sat and talked for a while until Pete's phone rang and he was needed somewhere else. They exchanged handshakes and gratitude again, then as Pete walked to the door he turned to Harvey and said, "Harvey, I promise you, I will not let you be exposed to any more danger if I can help it. If you get a glimpse of something uncomfortable or even something that just doesn't feel right, just call me. You have my private cell number, so call me night or day. I'll keep you updated on everything I know. Just be alert and trust no one."

As soon as Pete was gone, Harvey realized he needed to go get Velcro. No, he thought, *be steady. You need to get your guns and ammunition together. Velcro will be okay for the time being.*

On the drive back to Roberta's, Harvey wondered if he should even stay at her house. He certainly didn't want her involved, but he wanted her company, and, after that kiss, he felt like a teenager on his first date with the Prom Queen. Besides, she was silly smart which gave him chills just thinking about her.

He realized he needed to return her call anyway, so thought he would talk to her about it before he made the decision one way or the other. She would need to know what kind of danger he was in so she could decide whether to ride it out with him. He felt his anger rising at the thought that anything might come her way. One more thing for the villains to answer for.

That line of thinking reminded him to find a good shooting range and get back to practicing with his gun. It had been a while since he used it. He knew he was already a very good shot, but now he needed to become a great one. He had been around guns, shooting and hunting for most of his life so he felt very confident about carrying the weapon. He had a concealed permit, which was the first thing he got when arriving in Washington State and had taken every gun class, took safety class for both handguns and rifles but he was not sure about the firearms regulations. He made a note to check those out as well.

When he got to Roberta's, he let himself in with her key. Velcro was waiting for him right inside the door and greeted him with excitement. He greeted her, then did a quick look around the place to see that nothing was out of place and there had been no 'accidents'. She must have sat by the door all morning waiting for her master to return. She was such a good dog and oh, so smart.

While seeing to Velcro's needs, he realized it would be safer to get his car out of sight in the garage if possible. Roberta had a three-car garage and as far as he knew only had one car, so he thought there should be plenty of room. He went out the kitchen door to the garage and opened it from the inside. As he'd hoped, there was plenty of room for another car in the third bay. He grunted in appreciation that her garage was so neat and orderly. His was always full of junk.

He grabbed his keys d pulled the car into the third bay, and then closed the door. He'd need to ask Roberta for an opener if he was going to stay for a while, but at least if someone were looking for his car, they would not be able to see it from the street. In fact, even when the main double doors were open, you couldn't see the third bay, so the position was perfect.

Harvey looked around at every window, every opening, and even everything lying on the shelves to familiarize himself with his surroundings. It was something he learned as a kid growing up; to be always aware of things around you. One never knew when a natural disaster might happen, and you would need emergency supplies or an escape route. He even walked around the entire property and took note of where the neighbor's entrances were located. It was a very upscale neighborhood, so he figured most of the houses had alarms.

He had just finished his inspection when his phone rang. The noise startled him from his deep concentration. He pulled the phone out of his back pocket and saw it was Roberta. He had forgotten to call her back.

He answered the phone with a cocky, "Hey good looking'. What you up to?"

After a brief silence, Roberta said, "Harvey, I'm on speaker in my office."

He nearly dropped the phone out of his hand. "Ugh, I'm so sorry, Roberta," He sputtered, horrified by his gaffe. "I was obviously trying to be a smarty pants!"

"It's okay Harvey. It's just me and my assistant here. I hadn't heard from you and was concerned." Roberta picked up the receiver on the phone and said, "Okay now, you're off speaker and Lisa has gone to fetch some files for me."

"I apologize, Roberta. It's been one crazy morning. You'll never believe what I went through today.,"

"Goodness, Harvey, I can hear it in your voice. Are you okay?"

"Yes, I am now," Harvey replied. "You don't have to worry. We can talk about it when you get home. I've got a lot of work to do, so I thought we could figure out dinner when you get here."

"That's another reason why I'm calling you," she explained. "There's a new case that just popped up today. It's just an ordinary case but I need to go to complete an inspection and was wondering if you wanted to drive out with me. It's out in Silverdale and I'd like the company on the drive. But I understand if you have work."

"No, no," Harvey quickly responded. "I've already checked in with the office, so I'm just trying to get a jump on next week's trial date. I'd love to go with you. "

"That's great. I'm happy to say there's no murder involved with this one!" She gave a sort of half-laugh. "I'd like you see what my *normal* work is like. When I leave here, I need to go to the hospital and check on the babies, then I'll swing by and pick you up."

"Did I hear you say 'babies'?" Harvey asked.

"You sure did. Set of twins born in a garage then left on the floor wrapped in a dirty blanket. The neighbors kept hearing babies crying for a couple of days and nights. The house is well known for its drug activity. The story goes that the mom was high on something so went to the garage, delivered her own babies, went to the bathroom to clean up, then took off.

"Oh, man, are you kidding me?" said Harvey in pure amazement.

"No, I'm not kidding. The babies have pneumonia and are not doing well. And we don't know who the mom is or where she has taken off to," replied Roberta.

"Well, I think your story tops mine today. I just have to take care of Velcro, but I'll be ready whenever you get here Roberta," said Harvey. "Oh, by the way, I put my car in your garage. I'll explain later. I hope that's alright."

"Of course, you can! You could park it on the lawn if you wanted to. I'm just glad you've agreed to stay," she replied.

CHAPTER 18

ROBERTA SWUNG BY THE HOUSE AND PICKED UP HARVEY in her shiny white Infinity QX60. All the way to Silverdale, the two chatted non-stop. She was using the GPS since their location was well off the beaten path. Harvey could not keep from thinking about the night he drove down the back roads to get home when he found Anna. That was the night his life changed.

Without notice, the entry to a nice little neighborhood with kids playing and dogs barking appeared on their right and they turned in. The subdivision appeared to be a normal medium-income-level neighborhood. Roberta said that she could not understand why, of all the places, they would choose such a faraway place to do the drug business. She also couldn't figure out how a mother who had just delivered twins in a garage could just get up and walk away. Had she been on foot? Was she alone or did someone take her there and then drive her away? Was she even alive or was she lying somewhere in these dark wooded areas having bled to death? She sighed. It was her job to get to the bottom of this and unveil the truth.

Arriving at the house, the police, DEA, and the Sheriff's office people were still on site. She was surprised to see all the official cars, but the rest of the neighborhood was acting like it was a normal occurrence. The house and those around them were neat and orderly, but they could see that the lawns were unkempt, and each house showed some signs of neglect and wear.

"Do you want me to stay in the car?" Harvey asked.

"Absolutely not," she said, laughter dispelling her worry. "You've earned your way into this crime scene. You've proven you can probably handle it better than me!" she said, laughing out loud.

They entered the house and were assailed by the filth inside. There were roaches, rats, and mice running everywhere. Windows were broken and the back door teetered on its hinges. Dirty clothes were flung everywhere, lying amidst piles of booze cans and bottles in every corner of the house. Cigarette butts were squashed into the floors everywhere and dark piles that Harvey did not want to even think about were strewn around.

Worst of all was the stench that filled the house. The agents milling over the scene handed them masks to help with the smell.

Roberta took pictures of every room, especially where the babies were born. The afterbirth still lay on the floor of the downstairs bathroom. Blood was everywhere, leading a trail across the house and into the garage.

Roberta engaged in conversation with the DEA and local law enforcement as Harvey stepped outside. He could not even believe there was a house like this in this quiet, little neighborhood.

Within fifteen minutes, Roberta came walking very quickly out of the house, yanking off her mask and gasping for air. Harvey was leaning against the car and jumped up to meet her in the driveway. She was coughing and waving her hand back and forth in front of her face.

"Wow, the next time you ask me to accompany you on a call, remind me to decline the offer," Harvey said with a wry smile. They waited a few minutes longer for Roberta to catch her breath and get the smell of the foul house out of their minds.

On the way back, she told Harvey the details about what had apparently happened. The FBI and the police had done a good job of wrapping up the crime scene and had already spoken to neighbors on both sides of the house.

She had discovered that the FBI was called in because there were two crates of assault weapons and probably a couple hundred thousand fentanyl tablets found in the house. It seems that this house was used for storing larger deliveries of products from dealers and drug runners, including a few of the local addicts that lived there.

If the next-door neighbors had not reported the crying babies, they might never have found the place. It was a great cover spot; the criminals knew that the local police did not have the staff to engage in the on-going reports of drugs and crazy people coming and going day and night. The police could not act until there was clear evidence that a crime was taking place. The crying twins gave the authorities the cover they needed to move in.

The highway patrol heard the call when it first hit the airwaves, so they went to see if they could help out. This level of law enforcement officer was trained to identify drug carriers on the freeways, so knew the danger in drug houses They had seen just about everything in dealing with the operations of the Mexican cartel criminals. Many times, they had found children who had been riding in the trunk for hours with no care, no bathroom stops, no food or water. The cartels sell these children for sex to drops along the I-5 corridor all the way up to and through the Canadian border.

When the highway patrolmen heard the call, they knew that a small county precinct like Kitsap County would have very limited experience and protocol for dealing with traffickers and drugs. They feared that the well-meaning local officers would not appreciate the danger they were in without some backup. Roberta was thankful that the patrolmen were there and had notified the FBI.

At that time there was no lead on the mother or father to these twins. The neighbors all knew it was a drug house and had reported it repeatedly to local authorities who claimed they were unable to do anything. They had even contacted their local congressmen, city mayor, and city council but no one had offered help or a solution.

"Maybe I should have stayed in New York," Harvey said as he learned the enormity of the problem. "I don't think we have that much drug crime in our local neighborhoods."

"You might be surprised," she answered. "But you have to understand that the State of Washington is a far-left state that doesn't believe in laws and allows criminals to roam free. It's supported by the courts, the governor and especially the city council in Seattle."

"Pierce, Thurston, Clark and other large counties have a little better staff and have more trained people to deal with these adverse matters. I have a dream to create a resource center with more qualified staff to understand the profiles of these new types of criminals and how they operate. We still have local law enforcement, but they're down about 60% down in manpower. Honestly, the only reason the FBI or DEA gets involved is because of the guns and the amount of drugs they had stored. Still, I'm thankful they are involved. We get much more information from them, and they are so thorough that they make my job easier. The fact that babies – newborns – were involved raised another flag," she added.

"Well, let's put some distance behind us from this place and go home and I'll fix you a great meal!" proclaimed Harvey, happy that he had planned early. He had picked up a couple of chicken breasts, a rice pilaf mix, greens for a great salad, and a couple bottles of wine. He was ready to help let this beautiful woman relax while he pre-pared dinner.

Harvey was a good cook. He had been cooking for himself long before his wife died and he learned a lot of tricks from Cassie's sisters while they were caring for Cassie during her last months. He had needed to fill his mind with something other than suffering as he watched his wife die a little every day.

As they headed home, Roberta was interested in his 'busy' and 'unusual' day, as he had described it to her on the phone. Without hesitation, Harvey unpacked everything he had been through, start-ing at the market where he spotted his tail, through the police action, and up to the part where he had a gun held to his head. Roberta was in complete shock; during his story, Roberta reached over and put her hand on his knee, telling him how sorry she was that he had to go through all this.

As he was relating his adventure, Harvey's anger built up again at the people who had harmed Anna and were making his life so difficult. Yet he calmed down at Roberta's warm touch on his leg, awe-struck at how powerful her touch had been. He said to himself, "*Am I some kind of high school boy here with a crush?*" But he smiled at the thought and wanted to remember the feeling when he had a chance to recall the enchanting moment.

Velcro was waiting at the door from the garage to the kitchen when they arrived at Roberta's house. She wagged her tail and barked in greeting. Finally, her master was home again and so was her new friend.

CHAPTER 19

A S THINGS SETTLED DOWN IN THE NEXT FEW DAYS, Harvey continued to work closely on the case that he and Gunner had been assigned. When he finally felt it was safe and returned to his office downtown, Gunner came bounding in and flopped himself down on the comfortable client's chair. Gunner had never seen his friend so happy or so engaged with another human being, especially a woman, since losing his wife. Harvey didn't share many details, but he spoke of Roberta as if she were a goddess, with admiration, respect, and maybe even love pouring out of his mouth when he just spoke her name.

Harvey spent more time talking about Roberta's worst abuse cases than he did on the firm's multi-million-dollar case that was headed to trial. Although Harvey had made a real name for himself in corporate law, he did always take on a few smaller clients, often winning the cases against far more powerful corporations. It was easy for Gunner, and probably the other partners, to see that Harvey's passion was representing those who had a hard time getting heard. It was no surprise then that Harvey spent hours upon hours giving his critical views on Roberta's cases, some of which had been stuck in court for years. He had become Roberta's secret weapon and her accomplishments were off the charts.

Harvey was a good attorney and a great problem solver with an engineer-like mind to approach roadblocks from an angle that had never been tested or even thought about. It was if he could remove himself from reality and be like a drone looking at the problem from a wide global angle. Add this to his negotiation skills and the strategies he had learned from his late wife and it was like magic.

Gunner secretly worried that the senior partners would take offense at the constant distractions by their "awarding wining" attorney, but this was not true in this case. As the senior member of the firm told all the partners in their monthly Board Meeting, Harvey was bringing something this firm never had before Harvey's actions were enhancing the reputation of the firm with the press and the citizens of the city and state. In response, the partners even added new divisions to take on small yet more visible cases. This opened up an entirely different kind of law practice than they ever imagined, one that was not only popular, but also immensely profitable.

In short, Harvey proved to be an excellent find.

With her increased success rate, Roberta's position, which was already over several large counties, had been expanded statewide. The state even created a new position for her to head up its entire CPS division. While she loved her new position, she was still drawn to those cases that just didn't have all the correct factors. She occasionally stepped in on individual cases, giving advice and counsel on how to achieve the best for the child. Although CPS leaders did not like it, nor did the judges appreciate her involvement, no one could argue with her spot-on results.

Social workers were frightened of her. Not that they didn't admire her skill level, but she normally created more work, more investigation, and demanded more proof to ensure the child's best interest was being served. Many of the social workers came over to Roberta's system of doing things, going the extra mile to get their results. But some were just too lazy or too wounded by the previous system to find resolution by fighting for the children.

Every now and then Roberta would even jump into a case personally, usually where an infant had been beaten, or a child had been moved from home to home, or where parents were constantly letting down their responsibilities. Anna remained a driving force for their passions and she and Harvey spoke frequently about how just doing her job or just being a good citizen to stop and help someone in trouble had brought them together. Harvey continued to go on calls with her for special cases where crime was involved.

Meanwhile the mystery of Anna and her mother's murder was still active. Harvey kept in close contact with Pete who told him that one of the two guys they caught entering Harvey's house squealed like junkyard brakes. Sadly, that guy ended up somehow getting knifed in prison.

For a long time, there had been no threats against Harvey or his house, although the FBI warned him to stay alert. They still worried that catching the two 'small-timers' had brought too much attention to the organization so they had withdrawn for a while to let things cool off. The FBI also knew that the weapons and drugs were still missing and that the bad guys would not stop until they had retrieved their stash.

The surviving criminal was still behind bars for attempted murder, breaking and entering, possession of a stolen car, carrying an unregistered weapon, and a whole slew of other charges. Once his teammate was murdered, they put him in solitary to ensure his safety and even had him transferred to another state prison.

Roberta and Harvey were still seeing each other almost every night. Frequently when they were together, there would be a phone call to Roberta which would end up with her jumping in the car and going to either the scene of a crime or to the side of a child that had been severely harmed. She was always interested, particularly if a case had a crime connected. Many times, Harvey would accompany her.

If they were not dragged out for some drama, they spent their time at one of their homes, dining, playing with Velcro, or working side by side on their own cases. They each had their own sleeping spaces. It was not that they didn't love each other, even to the point of declaring their love out loud. Yet without talking about it, they both chose to hold back on sexual intimacy. They were as close as any married couple, but they wanted to hold onto their relationship's sanctity. It was if they realized that once they crossed that line, it would be game over. They feared if they ever gave all of themselves to another person, they would be opened to more hurt and pain.

There was never a dull moment between them. Each had huge caseloads to carry. Each continued to attend seminars and conferences that would help improve their skill level. But when they were together, for now, that seemed to be enough. They both knew the day would come when they could no longer resist each other – there had already been a few times when they almost crossed the line. For this moment in time, though, they were completely satisfied with their relationship, and each knew they loved each other more than life.

In the blink of a very busy eye, the holidays were just around the corner. Time had passed so fast. They had been together for ten months now and would not trade a minute of it. Now there were holiday parties, decorations for Christmas, and so many things to add to their already crazy lives. They were always exhausted. Even though the pressure had dropped off from the crimes that had brought them together, both Roberta and Harvey were running on an empty tank. They had not had one break since the night Anna was found.

Most of their time was spent at Roberta's house, since its closed garage and remote location felt safer to Harvey. But on a beautiful Saturday night when the rain had stopped, rare for winter on the Sound, they decided to spend the evening at Harvey's place. Velcro was always happy to be home, although Roberta's house was home to her now as well.

They were sitting wordlessly looking out at the water from the comfort of the large lounging couch. It was a little chilly, but they could feel the warmth of the fireplace behind them and the soft warm blanket that covered them.

The silence was broken when Velcro began growling deep in her throat. Harvey was alerted in an instant and jumped off the couch, heading towards his bedroom nightstand. In a moment, Harvey returned to the living room and grabbed his phone to dial Officer Pete's private number. As the line rang, he took Roberta by the hand and signaled for her to go into the hall coat closet, giving her instructions to stay still and not come out until he called her. Roberta was shocked and scared, used to being in control, but she saw the urgency in Harvey's eyes and did as he asked.

Pete picked up the phone and said, "Harvey, what's wrong?"

"I'm not sure but Velcro is growling toward the door. Roberta is here Pete."

Pete had only to hear the concern in Harvey's voice before he answered, "I'll have a unit out there in five minutes. Stay out of the line of fire Harvey," he ordered. "This time they might come in blazing. I'm on my way too, but I'm at least ten minutes out." Without waiting for a response, Pete hung up the phone and Harvey imagined him calling his officers as he raced to his own car. Harvey hoped they would be in time.

Velcro was ordered to remain still and quiet although her ears were perked up like radio antennas. She crouched down in a lying position with her head firmly squared on the door, mirroring her owner's gaze.

A gunshot from the patio rang through the house blowing out the window. Harvey could hear Roberta gasp and softly weep from the closet. He told Velcro to lay low and then doubled back to the bedroom and climbed out one of the windows.

Harvey crept around to the back patio in time to see the intruder enter the house. Through the window he could see Velcro run to the door to defend her territory and protect her master. The dog came up behind the shooter and jumped up to bite his arm. The man spun around to point his gun at Velcro just as Harvey pulled the trigger on his own gun, blowing the intruder's gun and the hand that held it off to the other side of the room.

Velcro continued her run through the broken glass to get to her master and Harvey picked her up with his empty hand; the other still had the gun pointed at the intruder's head. Through the intruder's whimpering, Harvey could hear a siren coming down his street. He breathed a sigh of relief. All his training and practice had paid off. In his anger, he would have rather killed the guy, but he also knew he had valuable information.

Harvey called Roberta to come out and open the door for the police. Before she could get to the front, he reconsidered and called for her to wait.

"Velcro," Harvey commanded. "Go check outside and see if anyone else is here." Velcro dashed outside and ran around the house just as the police were coming down the drive. When it was clear that the dog had spotted no other intruders, Harvey whistled a "come" command and she returned to the house.

"Now Roberta, slowly open the door," Harvey gently asked.

As she carefully opened the door, Velcro came flying back across the broken glass again and to her master's side. A police officer followed, gun aimed and cocked. The officer recognized Harvey right away and lowered his weapon. Meanwhile more officers came in through the front door to fill the scene. The first officer in said, "Well Harvey, see you're working on another case."

They quickly assessed the area and saw the wreckage of the window and the intruder lying on the kitchen floor, injured and whining like a baby. They cuffed him and dragged him out to their squad car just Pete's car came barreling along the front driveway. He jumped out and ran to the house.

When he saw everything was under control, Pete released the breath he had been holding for what seemed like the whole drive from his house. "What's up with you Harvey?" he said, more calmly than he felt. "Do we need to remodel your place again?"

After a warm handshake, Harvey saw that Roberta was standing in the corner shaking. He immediately put his gun down and moved to hold her close. For a moment, no one else was in the room.

He led Roberta to the couch and carefully covered her with the blanket that had been tossed on the floor. Velcro instantly went to be by her side, but Harvey saw that the dog's paws were bleeding and she had pieces of glass sticking to her feet. He lifted her gently and took her to the sink to pull the glass out and wash out her feet, then bandaged her feet with the first aid kit and carried her back to Roberta.

Velcro and Roberta had clearly just about had it, but Harvey told the story over and over as each police officer had a new slate of questions. After it was clear that the scene had been completely neutralized, the other officers went outside to check the property, leaving only Pete behind. The officer was irate that the gang had become active again and no one had bothered to notify him or his men.

Harvey looked around at the mess in his house. "Well, rain is coming," he said. "I guess I need to get this slider covered. I think my neighbor has some plywood in his garage. I'll going to go check."

Pete insisted that Harvey should stay in the safety of his home and went to get one of his men to talk to the neighbor. "They'll need to see if your neighbor had witnessed anything, anyway," he said stepping out into the cold darkness of the evening.

Harvey sat on the couch with his arm around the still shaken Roberta. Harvey contacted his security company, letting them know what had happened and he would put the alarm back on.

When the officer returned with his borrowed goods, Pete and Harvey put up the plywood as best they could. Then Harvey loaded the car with their computers and files and carried Velcro to the backseat. He shook hands again with Pete and promised to call him the next day, then he returned to the house to lovingly lead Roberta still wrapped in her blanket to the front. When she had settled in, he went back to retrieve his gun and ammunition and turn on the alarm.

The ride to Roberta's house was filled with shocked silence. Velcro was lying down in the back seat since it hurt her to stand on her paws. Harvey made a mental note to dress the wounds better before bed and make sure the cuts were not so deep as to require a trip to the vet.

Roberta was just silent, which was very unusual for her, but Harvey decided he would wait until he got to her house to engage in conversation. When they reached Roberta's house, he circled the block several times looking for any signs of someone following him or any strange, parked car on the street. By now he was very familiar with the cars that belonged to this neighborhood, and he felt he could spot something out of place.

Looking in his rear-view mirror he saw a car slowly following him two car lengths behind. He had seen it before but told himself it was nothing and he was overreacting. It's reappearance so soon after this new attack made him more than nervous. He noticed it was a dark sedan but couldn't make out the make and model. He sped up till he could no longer see the car's headlights, then took a quick turn out of the neighborhood to the right, parking the car under a hanging tree and turning off his lights. Velcro raised her head to see what was up, but Harvey slid down in his seat until he saw the car speed past without even noticing him on the side of the road.

As the car passed by, Harvey looked into its window to see if it was the same guys who had been following him before. Instead he thought he saw Sheriff Bloom. The driver had the same profile and the big shoulders and body. At first, he tried to rationalize Bloom's presence, but then he thought, *wait a minute, if that was the Sheriff, he had no business being in Gig Harbor except to watch him.* Harvey argued with himself back and forth for a few minutes, finally scolding himself for even thinking such a thing. *Bloom is loved by his deputies and his town,* he thought. *He's probably the most trusted man in the whole area. I'm way off base here. Get a grip, Harvey.*

Thankfully, Roberta was still in a daze and didn't even notice. He made sure the car was out of sight and did a quick U-turn to return to the house.

He pulled into the garage, closing the door before he got out of the car. Roberta's alarm was set too but Harvey knew the code and opened the door, turning on the lights to the halls and family room. Roberta sat in the car staring out the window, not even seeming to recognize where she was.

Harvey picked up Velcro and carried her to the family room, putting her in her special place on the couch. He returned to Roberta still sitting in the car and trembling in fear. As he reached his hand out to her, she said, "If I feel like this, how must children feel when they're in harm's way?"

Harvey fell more in love than ever, astounded that even in her shocked state this amazing woman should be thinking of 'her kids' first and foremost. He decided it was best to talk about the children in peril rather than what they had just been through. Let her internalize the events and reach out to a situation where she might have control. The violence that they had just suffered was totally outside of her wheelhouse.

CHAPTER 20

AFTER THEIR VERY ROUGH EVENING, ALL THREE OF them fell asleep on the couch. They were awakened by the howl of wind and rain as the threatened storm raced through the Peninsula. It was the two-week mark until Christmas.

Harvey and Roberta had finally been able to talk through the events before drifting off in each other's arms, yet they both felt like they were hung over without the benefit of spirits. Harvey reached over and checked Velcro's feet. She appeared to be doing better, her wagging as she acted like she wanted to go outside even though it was windy and rainy.

Harvey let Velcro out and started a pot of coffee. They never did eat anything the night before, so he put a couple of English muffins in the toaster and filled Velcro's water and food bowls. Roberta also had recovered considerably from the night before and seemed perkier and much more 'in the moment'. They agreed to hash the evening over one more time and then put it to bed for a later discussion when they knew more.

They both agreed how horrible and scary it was, but each knew they had lost an entire evening of work as well. They both had court dates coming up, so their time was critical. Then they laughed that they were most concerned about work during the horrible occurrence.

Harvey planned to contact both of their security companies to have cameras installed around the outside of both houses, along with movement flood lights. He did not, under any circumstances, want to be taken by surprise again. Roberta thought this was overkill, but she decided to humor Harvey and let him build his fort.

It was a rainy Sunday as they both nestled in to enjoy the silence of the day. Velcro was catching up on her sleep and the two adults were enjoying the peaceful afternoon knowing how busy their weeks were going to be.

Roberta's phone rang broke the silence. She answered and said nothing else for a few moments while the other party talked. "No," she said finally, "I'm glad you called. I'll be right there."

Completely taken by surprise, Harvey said "You're going to do what?" He immediately started pleading his case about their horrible evening before and the storm coming in, but she was determined. He followed her into the bedroom while she changed clothes, trying to get her to change her mind. When she was all prepared to leave, Roberta explained why she had to go out.

"There's a baby alone in a seedy motel – a well-known druggie hangout – and there's no mother or father in sight. The child kept crying until motel employees finally called the police. They found a newborn, not more than a few weeks old, wrapped in a blanket on top of the nasty bed cover. There was a diaper bag, of sorts with a few diapers and a couple of premade bottles but no sign that anyone had changed or fed the baby within the last few days. No address, no identification, no nothing. It's Sunday and the social worker on call has the 'flu' and can't get out of her house. She was crying on the phone but couldn't even leave her bathroom because of diarrhea and vomiting. She tried to contact her supervisor but couldn't reach her. Even the supervisor's supervisor was out of contact. But the law says the police have to hold the baby in the motel until CPS arrives on the scene."

She gave him a quick kiss on the cheek, "I'm sorry to break up or peaceful recovery, Harvey, but I have to go. There's no one else."

"I'm going with you, then," Harvey firmly stated. "You're not going out there alone. I've been to scenes like this before, remember?"

"Well, go get dressed then and be quick about it," she scolded, smiling.

As Harvey jumped into his clothing, he decided that it was best for him not to be angry or frustrated, but to support her in her duties. By the time he stepped back out into the hallway, he knew he was doing the right thing. He turned off the coffee and told Velcro to stay, that they would be back later. Velcro seemed to be the happiest in the room; she didn't have to go out in the storm.

When Roberta entered the room, Harvey immediately went to her, held her face and kissed it, saying, "I'm so sorry, Roberta. I should never doubt or question you. You always make the right decisions."

Roberta answered, "I'm sorry too, Harvey. It's just been a lot lately. I'm glad you're going with me. I really need your company."

• • •

Despite the storm, there was little traffic on the road, and they arrived at the fleabag motel in short order. The rain and wind had died down to the regular Washington State mist. The dreary day did nothing to liven up the location, although Harvey was sure that the place would have looked dismal even on the brightest of sunny days. As they stepped out of the car, they could see half-drowned homeless people and soaked drug addicts sheltering under the wings of the motel. Rank filth met them again, although not quite as bad as the last stop.

They climbed the chipped staircase and entered the room where an officer was rocking and holding the baby. He immediately stood up and held the infant at arm's length towards Roberta.

Roberta smiled and put her hands up. "Oh, would you please give the baby to him?" She pointed to Harvey and the puzzled policeman shrugged but complied. "I have some questions and would like to see the reports you are filing," she explained to both men. "I also need to take a few photographs."

Harvey willingly took the baby in his arms, cooing softly to it.

"Now, is this where the baby was lying when you found her?" she asked.

"No," answered the officer. "That is, I didn't find her although this is the room where she was found. She's a girl by the way, although we have no idea if she has a name yet or anything. Officer Martinez found her and called it in. I was the only one of us with experience in holding a newborn. The others went to question the people in the other rooms."

He realized that he was missing something. "I'm Sergeant Mize," he introduced himself proudly.

"Thanks," Roberta said as she introduced herself. "Let me ask you a few questions if you don't mind."

While Roberta began her investigation in her most official manner, Harvey was holding the tiny little baby in his arms. This was probably the first newborn he had ever held, his mind rushed back to Anna and how weird holding her had felt at first. He was reluctant to sit down at all since everything was so dirty but in the end, he decided the baby would be more comfortable in his lap, so he took the Sergeant's chair. Hopefully, all the germs would be on the policeman's pants and not Harvey's. He chuckled at himself.

The newborn was sleeping, and Harvey thought she was the most beautiful baby he had seen. As soon as he sat down, though, the child began to squirm and he started to panic. Why was the baby squirming? Was he supposed to do something different? At that moment, the little baby opened her eyes and looked directly at Harvey. His heart melted in a great moment of joy. Then he began to wonder what was going to happen to her. Where would they take the baby? Who could ever be good enough to keep an angel like this?

He decided to be brave and talk to her. He knew nothing about the child except that she seemed to trust him for the moment. He held her out in front of him hoping to see the baby a little better, then rocked her gently and began singing "Cats in the Cradle". *Gee, is this the only song I know?* He thought. But it did the trick. She closed her eyes and went back to sleep.

Roberta completed what interviews she had to do with the officers on the scene. She thanked each of them graciously and went back into the room where Harvey was holding the baby.

"Well, Mr. Waggoner, I think I've seen this before," she said with a smile. "Do you always capture the hearts of such a young audience?"

CHAPTER 21

A T THAT INSTANT, A SOAKED AND SMELLY WOMAN WHO appeared so high she could barely stand looked in the door and said, "What are you doing with my baby?"

The color peaked in Harvey's face as he glared at this apparition. *Who was this pitiful woman, anyway,* he thought. *She can't even stand up without holding on to a door. No way, lady, are you getting this baby back.* Harvey tightened his hold on the infant, Roberta saw what was going on and needed to stop this, but first she needed information from this woman who claimed to be this newborn's mother.

Roberta took control of the situation and gently led this woman outside, signaling Harvey to get in the car. Harvey grabbed whatever bag was on the bed and cautiously made his way to the car while Roberta and the woman had their backs to him and the baby. He held his breath in hopes the tiny child would not make a sound until they got in the car.

Fifteen minutes later, Harvey saw the woman appear in the doorway flailing her hands in the air and shouting. The police officer waiting to take her into custody was sitting in his vehicle until he could lock up the crime scene. He could see they were heating up so he got out of the car. When he approached, the agitated woman started screaming and hitting the officer so he cuffed her and put her in the back seat. Roberta assured her that her baby (if it was her baby) would be safe until things could be sorted out. She quickly walked to the car and slid into the passenger's seat. With her phone in hand, she began trying to reach her favorite "I need you immediately" foster parents that could take the baby on short notice.

Harvey looked at her with a question on his face. "So, Roberta, do you want me to drive with this child in my lap or would you prefer to hold it?" he said with a smile.

Roberta smiled back and took the baby in her lap, putting the infant's little body next to her chest and locking them both in with the seat belt. She was frustrated with herself that she didn't have a safety seat in the car, but this was an emergency, and she didn't have the time to go to her office and pick one up. They would be driving only a few blocks, but Roberta reminded Harvey to drive safely, that they had precious cargo in the car.

After a few failed calls, she finally reached Miss Lilly who was always a life saver in emergencies. She had been Anna's foster mother as well. The rain had started up again so Roberta said, "Since we're downtown why don't we swing by my office so I can get paperwork started before morning. I'm betting this is going to be a tough case."

Within a few minutes, they were pulling into the building parking lot. Roberta took her security badge out of her purse and they headed to her office.

The guard greeted Roberta fondly as they stepped on the elevator. "Good evening, Ms. McEniry. It's nice to see you, but at this hour on a weekend right before Christmas, maybe not so good. Right?" He gave Roberta a broad grin.

"You know my cases don't always recognize time and holidays, Matt." They both nodded grimly as the elevator door closed. Harvey was not surprised at the high regard Roberta was shown. He knew she was quite a woman.

"Harvey, why don't you hold the baby in the guest chair while I make a few calls and check a few things out?"

"My pleasure," he responded, giving the baby a little squeeze. "You do know this feels like a déjà holding this tight to this baby while you and I are together." He made a face as he sniffed. "Maybe better start by changing her diaper first though."

"Good idea," she chuckled. "But there's only one more in the bag, so I hope you know what you're doing, partner."

Roberta's investigation took about an hour. She was able to confirm that the woman they had met had definitely delivered a baby. Also, Roberta found that she was already in the system and had an assigned Social Worker for her other four children, also not in her care. There was a slew of horrible accusations listed against the woman, but each child reportedly had a different father, supposedly. The number of Dads just kept getting longer, Roberta thought with grim humor.

She finished her calls and paperwork and then they headed for Miss Lilly's house, which was not too far away. Miss Lilly was one of the most special women she had worked with in the foster care system. She had been widowed a long time, and she was primarily used for emergencies until the courts had done their intake, social work had been assigned, and the case was on record. Miss Lilly never wanted to adopt children, but she would keep anyone that needed a place to call home, whether for a few days or for weeks on end. Babies, especially newborns, were her specialty. She had a background as a nurse and continued to stay on top of the most recent knowledge regarding newborn care. She never turned down a request to help a child. There were times when she ended up with two or three for the intake process. She was like the secret grandmother for all the children who needed care at a moment's notice. Roberta didn't know what she would do without the woman.

Miss Lilly was standing in the doorway when Roberta and Harvey pulled up. She greeted Roberta and Harvey warmly and then enfolded the infant girl in a warm hug, cooing and kissing her as she took her in her arms. Roberta and she talked briefly, but Miss Lilly really needed no instructions. She knew the system. Roberta would make sure the baby stayed with Lilly until the courts had settled and found a good foster home. They both knew that this case was not going to end soon, so Roberta promised to look into a foster home or maybe an adoption resource. It was always hard to move infants around from place to place. The first few months in a child's life are so critical.

Roberta was all for giving the parents a chance to get their 'stuff' together to parent their own children, but in this case, with the mother's history of inability to even function as a human being, she thought that this baby might have got out of the fire pit just in time.

As they drove home, Roberta leaned over and kissed Harvey on the cheek. "Harvey, you're the most special person I've ever met. I'm constantly amazed at how compassionate you are and how much love you show these at-risk children. I'm so thankful that our paths crossed. all those months ago. You mean the world to me. I couldn't have faced tonight without you." She sniffed as a tear rolled down her cheek.

It has defiantly been a rough couple of days, Harvey thought. He wondered how she could see the horrific drama that afflicted unwanted and abused children every day and continue to be so positive. He smiled at her to give her as much courage and support as he could offer.

Back at her house, they were greeted by Velcro, who was so happy to see them, but was also ready to eat and go outside. Harvey instantly performed his dog duties then went into the kitchen to whip something up to eat. He poured them both a glass of wine and, despite knowing that they were not completing their planned work for the evening, they just sat comfortably on the couch and unwound together from the last trauma of the last few days.

When she continued to work on the case that week in her office, Roberta discovered that the mother had given birth to the child in a free clinic and then grabbed the baby and snuck out. There was a warrant out for her arrest on this and multiple other charges. Now the courts would be adding child abandonment. This was going to be a very long and involved case indeed.

CHAPTER 22

I T WAS THE WEEK BEFORE CHRISTMAS NOW AND BOTH Roberta and Harvey were struggling. Finding the Christmas spirit was very difficult in both their lines of work even in normal circumstances. For Roberta, the season always made the tragedy of family abuse seem even worse. In Harvey's world, everyone was trying to wrap things up in court before the courts shut down for the holidays. When people rush, things are missed, which made him even more crazy. Many times, though, other people's blunders gave him an edge. Harvey knew how high-powered attorneys operated. They wanted to do whatever it took to get the case closed or delayed so they could spend the holidays on white sand, blue sky, and tall cool drink in their hand! Harvey was a master at taking advantage of his opposition's loss of concentration.

This year, though, it was Harvey who had trouble focusing. Not only was his mind constantly drawn to thoughts of Anna. It was difficult for him to forget the newborn baby too. While she had not been as abused as Anna, she was still in a pitiful position and his heart had completely been saturated by this tiny little girl in their brief time together. He wanted to be her protector and provider, to give her the good life her innocence deserved.

He caught himself thinking about her at the office, his desk littered with the briefs that he was supposed to be studying. *What the heck am I doing?* he thought, as he jumped up from his chair. *These aren't my children. The situations aren't my battles and aren't mine to dream about!* He shook his head to try to clear his confusion.

As he moved to drink some more coffee, Roberta called him on his mobile phone. She told him that she had received a call from a very dear friend of hers who was a Court Appointed Special Advocate (CASA). The woman, Kelly, had intervened in cases Roberta had worked in the past and they had become very good friends over the years. Kelly and Roberta shared similar backgrounds: they had both had traumatic childhoods and had both gone through messy divorces.

Kelly's background was in finance; she had an MBA, which made her valuable to many of the institutions in the Northwest. She also had come to the Seattle area from the Midwest, another reason to become instant friends when they met at a party one night years ago. It made sense, of course. People with similar backgrounds always seem to find each other and share their lives through storytelling over a glass of wine after work. Roberta had talked her into being a CASA to help her heal. Since Kelly had an unbelievable spirit of giving, she decided to try it and, ten years later, she was loved and treasured by most of the social workers in the department.

Kelly had chatted with Roberta for a while, and then delivered her bombshell question. "When exactly did CPS change the rules for placing an infant with someone who was not vetted and allow a so-called 'relative' to pick up and transport a child?" she had asked.

Kelly could not see the shock on Roberta's face, but heard the urgency in her voice as the CPS head asked, "What rules are you talking about, Kelly?"

Kelly spent the next ten minutes telling her how the social worker on a case she was working did not vet the 'third cousin' of a newborn, and never notified her, as the CASA assigned to the case, about any change in the care giving arrangement. The baby in this case was only about four weeks old and the adoptive foster parents were broken-hearted and confused about this transfer being made in a day. As far as Kelly knew, the courts had never worked that fast for a replacement, and she knew of no motions that were or of anyone who had been notified. She only learned about it when ~~the from~~ the foster mom called crying about losing a child they had been told would be adoptable. The social worker had even allowed the cousin to pick the baby up at the foster parent's home, something that was never permitted.

Kelly had been unable to get in touch with the social worker for more than a week. The caseworker would never return Kelly's calls, and neither would the supervisor.

"I know how the courts favor relatives for children, especially babies," Kelly had continued to say, "but my goodness, this happened over night, and I could find no one to talk to me about it. Additionally, I don't believe the social worker even had an inspection done at the cousins' house, and the foster parents told me that they picked the baby up in a broken-down car filled with other people. According to the foster mom, the cousins smelled nasty."

Roberta was beyond angry. She had explained as calmly as she could force herself that there had been no changes in the law or in the protocol for children. She tried not to let her anger come through her voice because that would make her friend even more upset. She had Kelly provide her with the names of the people involved and began researching reports on the social worker.

With a few calls and little bit of research in the system, Roberta had found the child's parents had outstanding warrants issued, and there had been no background check or inspection of the so-called cousin on the records. She also discovered that the baby had been placed on an Indian Reservation at the tip of the peninsula in Forks. This gave her no authority over the case. The situation was about as ugly as it could get.

Since it was just mid-morning, Roberta had suggested they both hop in the car and drive out to do their own inspection and check on the baby. Kelly thought that was a great idea, asking for about a half an hour to move her schedule around. Kelly was excited since she had not had any time with her good friend in several months. It was Christmastime and who better to spend a few days with?

Roberta was calling to let Harvey know she would be out of pocket for the day and possibly more. He told her he would have dinner ready when she returned but asked her to keep in touch so he would not worry. He did not like the idea of Roberta diving two hours for something that someone else could do, but he knew Roberta and that nothing he could say would sway her from her mission.

Almost thirty minutes to the minute, Roberta swung by Kelly's office and picked her up. The two began discussing the case, but Kelly was much more interested in this "new guy" that Roberta spoke about so lovingly on the phone. The two crossed the Narrows Bridge and headed west toward their destination, giggling and catching up on each other's lives. Neither of them had a clue what they were going to face. Sometimes, in cases like this, it's easier to just go with the flow.

After a long but beautiful drive, they reached the town that was their destination, but addresses were not easy to find with so few street signs. They finally stopped at a little store and asked for directions to the Indian reservation. When the clerk looked at them like they had asked for the address to hell, Roberta began to get concerned.

The further they drove the less signal they had on their cell phones. By the time they saw the entrance to what they thought must be the reservation, there was no signal at all. Roberta's concern continued to deepen. Even high-spirited Kelly was taken aback by what they were seeing. As they drove slowly into the village reservation, there were no signs and no addresses at all. Every road was lined with groups of young men, standing in the street gawking at them as they passed by.

They made a circle of each street, then noticed a house at the edge of the settlement with a small handmade sign out front that read, "The Council meets here." Roberta decided to go in by herself, leaving Kelly to watch the car. Surrounded by a curious gaggle of gawkers, Kelly instantly locked the doors and began to pray. The entire situation felt unsafe and freaky. She and Roberta were obviously not tribe members. What if they were not allowed here?

After what felt like hours but was less than five minutes, Roberta came out of the hovel. Her face was set in an angry scowl. Kelly quickly unlocked the doors and then relocked again as soon as Roberta was safe inside.

"There was definitely a council meeting in there they all stared at me like I was an alien," she reported. "There was a lady who seemed to be the head of the group and she knew exactly who I was talking about. She said we needed to head down the street four houses on the left. She didn't look happy that we were looking around. She asked if there was a problem but I told her this was just routine, unscheduled visit by Child Protective Service, something we always do. I don't know if she bought it or not, but at least they gave me directions and let me come out."

Roberta put the car in gear but held the brake on and turned to her friend. "Kelly," she said, "you should let me go in and do this on my own. CASAs aren't paid enough for this kind of visit." They both laughed, knowing that CASAs were volunteers.

"Not on your life Missy," Kelly answered, shaking her head of bright red hair. "This is my case, too. No way am letting you make any sort of sacrifice alone. Besides, I'm not staying out in this car with those boys standing there and glaring at me like I'd done something!"

Roberta shrugged and nodded then drove just a little way down the street confusing the guys who were following them on foot. The group of men laughed a little as the car pulled to a stop so close to where they had been parked. The two friends looked at each other like they were not going to make it out alive, then took deep breaths and climbed out of the car, not daring to look at the welcoming party. Some of the pack came over where they had stopped and sat down on the trunk of their car.

"Okay, let's do this" Roberta said. She grabbed her purse and reached for the vial of pepper spray that she always carried with her. She nodded as Kelly seemed to be doing the same thing. Roberta reared up to her full height which seemed to tower over most of the young men around them. Squaring her shoulders, she crossed the road to the small, shabby house that had been pointed out to them.

They found the front screen door torn and hanging by one hinge. Roberta knocked on the door lightly and it flew open at her touch. They both stood there, wondering if they should go in or get out of there. While they stood, an older lady came from around the corner. Roberta identified who she was. The woman gave a quick shrug and invited them to follow her inside.

The woman led them through the house and directly into the kitchen. When they were inside that room, she signaled for them to wait and stepped back out into the house.

As the two warriors stood in the kitchen, shivering from the cold inside the house, they both wished that they had thought their plan through a little deeper. It was so cold inside that Roberta was not sure the house even had heat. Each side of the sink was filled with dirty dishes and roaches crawled everywhere. Whatever flooring had once been there had either been pulled up or had just disintegrated, showing the packed dirt underneath. A cat was walking across the dinner table eating the scraps of whatever was left on the table.

At last, the lady entered the room and said, "Come on in and have a seat. Excuse the mess. We've been working this week."

The woman took the edge of the couch closest to the kitchen since what appeared to be a teenage boy was sprawled out on the rest of the couch. Roberta carefully made her way further into the room where she spotted the tiny infant lying motionless at the far end of the couch with the boy's feet and filthy socks resting on it. The woman followed Roberta's gaze and cackled, "Oh don't mind the boy. He's always taking a nap!" She slapped the boy on his rump and laughed out loud, but she made no effort to make the boy get up or move his feet away from the baby.

Their host seemed to be in a friendly, chatty mood, so Roberta asked if she could pick up the baby. "Sure, help yourself," the woman said. Kelly came up beside Roberta and saw the baby with a gasp.

"Oh, don't worry about her," the lady said, still giggling. "That baby sleeps through everything. We just got back from working. We're guides, you know. We fish and hunt, and just have a good time because that's our business! What a great life, huh?".

"Who takes care of the baby when you're out on your guide trips. Or do you take her with you?" asked Roberta.

"Oh hell, lady, we don't take no baby into the woods. She'd freeze her ass off! We leave her here with the kids. "Little Pete" here," she said, slapping the boy across the head. "He's 16 and his sister is 12. They can do anything. We have a four-year-old too, but that kid does nothing but play! If they need something, any of the people around here are glad to help." She sounded almost proud to be leaving a less than two-month-old baby with kids.

When Roberta picked up the child, she could smell dirty diapers. At first the baby seemed like she might be dead, but Roberta could see small movements that reassured her. Everything on her, including her blankets, was dirty and had dog hair all over it. The child even has dog hair on her face and in her mouth. Her face was crusted over with spilled milk and dry, flaky dirt and skin. She had a terrible, red rash, probably from filth and fleas.

The lady jumped up from her seat and said, "You might as well come with me and I'll show you her bedroom."

Everything in this house was filthy. But in the 'baby's room', a large, beautiful crib stood out as shiny and new. The rest of the furniture in the room, a broken-down bed and a nightstand, were covered in dirty adult clothes.

The woman patted the crib with pride. "The whole rez came together to give us this crib," she explained, giving another wild laugh. "It's the best piece of furniture in the house." Even this treasure had dirty baby clothes and a bunched-up blanket stuffed on top of the stained mattress. Roberta squeezed the small child harder against her. *How had the infant survived all this?* she wondered. *Living in the streets would be cleaner.*

They made their way back to the living area where the teenager was still asleep. When the old lady had settled back onto the crowded couch, Roberta decided she would dig a little deeper.

Roberta asked the woman why she was keeping the baby. Had anyone explained the rules of guardianship to her? The woman fixed her face in an angry sneer. "Rules?" she spat. "What are you talking about? I got a call from this distant cousin I hadn't heard from in years saying she was in trouble with the law. She asks me if I would take her baby for her. You CPS guys were all over her to straighten up and she wasn't ready for that."

"So, you're telling me you didn't get an opportunity to meet with the social worker?" Roberta asked.

"No, not yet. The woman on the phone said she'd get in touch later, but it's been about a month now. I was just trying to help out so my cousin wouldn't lose her kid," the woman said, a note of uncertainty creeping into her bluster. "Is there anything I need to do?"

"Well, one thing I would request is not to leave the baby unattended until I can help by getting you more information," Roberta said, not wanting the woman to think she was in trouble and possibly run.

Roberta knew she had no authority on the reservation. She was already lining up in her head what she would do from here. She looked up to Kelly, who was almost in tears, and gently put the baby back down on the dirty couch as far away from the boy's stinky feet socks as possible.

They thanked the woman for her kind hospitality and left the dirty house with the baby still at the mercy of this woman and her family. She even said a bullet prayer in her mind to God to please watch over the little girl until she could get help.

Once they got back in the car, the young males began moving closer and closer. Both Roberta and Kelly were nervous, ready to use their pepper spray if they tried to get in the car. Roberta locked the doors and started the engine and the boys split up and surrounded the car on all sides.

After a menacing few moments, the boys started to move towards the side doors and windows. As soon as they cleared the front of the car, Roberta stepped on the gas, tearing off so fast she did not care if she struck anyone or not. In the rear-view mirror, she could see the boys laughing and jeering at them. "Run, white woman, run!" they screamed at the retreating car.

They had to drive almost twelve miles before they had a good enough signal to make a phone call. Roberta pulled into the parking area of a small store and gas station and got on the phone. Kelly also called her supervisor to give the whole story so CASA could officially file a complaint.

Roberta called the attorney assigned to this division but was told by a harried receptionist that he was unable to take her call despite how urgent it was. She knew this attorney well, a very lazy blowhard. She knew all the rumors about his affairs with his various administrative assistants, so assumed he was off "shacking up" somewhere. Word travels fast in a small division.

Frustrated, Roberta called her own assistant to have her prepare documents for moving the child. Then she called Harvey.

Harvey could hardly believe how awful the situation she described with, although he had already seen that and far worse on their visits together. He told her he knew of an attorney who had a connection with the Indian tribes. Granted, all the tribes were different, but at least he could get information as to how to get this child removed as quickly as possible.

If Roberta had not stepped in to help her friend, the case would probably still be in someone's voice mail. But Kelly's supervisor got the ball moving by petitioning the court to remove the child. The CASA's end moved very quickly. They were the heroes here. A call had already been made to the police, who in turn contacted the tribe police council describing the deplorable conditions this infant had been placed in on their land. Meanwhile, Roberta and Kelly headed back to Tacoma to see what other buttons they could push for more urgency. Since it was Roberta who was the one pushing, things moved a little quicker. On top of all the authorities she contacted, Roberta also told her assistant to have the social worker in her office by the time she got back there. No excuses would be accepted.

Harvey called her back in short order but had nothing to offer her yet than what she and Kelly had already covered themselves. He told her that he was so disturbed by this case that he could hardly think about his own work. He planned to get over to Roberta's house to be on stand-by if he were needed.

As Harvey was packing up his gear, Gunner came into his office asking him why he looked so stressed and why he was leaving early with another day in court tomorrow. Harvey laid out what had taken place with Roberta. Gunner was blown away, not just from the story but also by the level of involvement and concern Harvey was showing.

"Harvey," said Gunner, crossing his legs and snuggling down in the beautiful leather chair, "you are really tied in knots, dude. Have you totally lost interest in the case here or are you just worried about Roberta?"

Harvey paused for a moment and looked deep into his friend's eyes as if he might find the answer to the question there. Finally, he responded, "Both Gunner. I am more than worried about Roberta since we've been through some pretty deep crap these last few days. Even she has a breaking point. I want to be there for her because I love her."

Gunner had never heard Harvey say anything like that since he married Cassie. He was about to comment but Harvey interrupted him.

"Hold on a minute, Gunner. I'm not finished yet," Harvey proclaimed. "I'm really tired of representing these wealthy buffoons suing the small guy and creating a path of dead bodies along the way. These guys are just suing to massage their egos about how great they are. I'm sick and tired of it." Gunner tried to speak again but Harvey held his hand up. "Wait. Just wait. I've been thinking about this for a long time. It's not just Roberta, it's me too. When I was studying to be a lawyer, all I wanted to do was work for kids like me and Roberta, who had a hard time growing up with parents who were focused on everything but being a parent. I only went into corporate law to satisfy Cassie. I mean it was the only way I could impress her, so I put my dreams aside. But honestly, I've never gotten over it.

"These last few months with Roberta and her unbelievable cases has shown me there are millions of children out there having to make their own way or stand up for themselves. No one fights for them, especially in this state! All these kids want is a secure home to come home to. They just want to be loved, be a part of a family again. Instead, they're tossed around by a broken-down social services network, broken promises, broken addicted parents, and a bunch politically motivated attorneys and judges. It eats at me, Gunner, it really eats at me." He slumped back, exhausted from sharing his heart.

"Well, Harvey," Gunner said, standing up out of his chair. "I won't hold you back. 'I'll do anything I can to help you achieve your dream. I got your back, buddy. Just tell me what you need me to do." Gunner reached over to pat his friend on the back and then headed back to his own office.

CHAPTER 23

B Y THE TIME ROBERTA GOT TO HER OFFICE, EVERY-
thing was in motion to remove the infant. Now they were just
waiting on the tribal council to give permission for the child to
be picked up. In her mind she recognized it could take time with the
tribe. They danced to their own timelines.

She met with the social worker who had been assigned the case.
The woman did nothing but weep, saying that she was overworked
with too many cases, and that she was exhausted by it all. When she
found out the entire story, she felt even worse. It is very common that
social workers get burned out. They are asked to carry the heaviest
weight on their shoulders and watch the show from the front seats.
They are grossly underpaid for the hours they spend and the some-
times-dangerous situations they are thrown into, all the while trying
to satisfy their supervisors and the laws and keeping the children's
best interests at heart. Dropping the ball by not doing proper inspections are the first things to suffer.

Roberta immediately ordered a review of every case the woman
had. The process was going to be ugly for the social worker. Although

Roberta really wanted to fire her on the spot, the CSA attorney said she could not do that since there had never been any negative reports on the woman's work. Roberta decided that she was going to make an example of this social worker and called for an urgent division wide meeting the following Monday. It was inexcusable for occurrences like this to happen on her watch.

At 8:00 that night, she was almost out the door for home when her office phone rang. She almost didn't answer since she was completely exhausted mentally and physically. As it turned out she was glad she did. The attorney from CASA reported that he had just heard from the tribe's counsel, and they were picking up the child themselves. Once they saw the filth that this infant was living in, the Tribal Police would not let this child suffer further harm. The tribe's counselor was embarrassed and apologized for not keeping better track of their reservation. In fact, they were making changes to inspections in the village. They would take the baby to the hospital in the town about 15 miles from the reservation and someone could pick her up there.

Roberta immediately sat down and put things in motion for the baby to be picked up and taken to a safe home overnight until she could find placement. She was mad at everyone now, the social workers, supervisors, of course, the attorney for the department, and especially the judge who all allowed an infant of this age to move to a living situation that had not had not been inspected. He, too, was just trying to lighten his load and probably didn't even notice that none of these protocols had been followed.

She pulled up at her house about 9:00 PM and found Harvey close to frantic from not hearing from her. He had not wanted to bother her with a call either. He heard the garage door open and close as Velcro began barking, knowing their friend was coming home.

Harvey was standing in the family room as she entered from the garage door. He looked at her with deepest compassion as tears began to flow down her cheeks. Harvey grabbed her and held her close for a few minutes, listening to her sobbing, but saying nothing.

Finally, she dropped her purse and messenger bag to the floor and Harvey said gently, "Well, girl, it sounds like you had one crappy day. But I've got a nice very nice glass of wine poured for you. Sit down on the couch, take your shoes off, try to relax." He went into the kitchen to get her the wine. "By the way, I stopped by your favorite Italian restaurant and picked up some chicken fettuccine and a small salad for supper. Don't worry about anything. Let's just talk." He looked at her lovingly as she rubbed her eyes. "If you want to, that is."

After a long period of silence, Roberta finally began to relax and start talking about her day. Harvey wanted to hear about everything. He had found out from his attorney friend that the tribe's counsel is the law of the land on the reservation and that it would take their permission to do anything. After all that, though, Roberta found out that the child had no Indian blood in her; her "cousin" was not even related to her. The mom knew how to work the social service system, though. She knew that being a part of an Indian tribe spoke volumes in child custody cases, but the "third cousin" was really just a friend she met years ago during high school.

At last, they got to a place where Harvey could warm up the dinner and they could sit at the table talking with ease about other things. As they prepared for bed, Harvey realized that tonight he did not want to sleep in bed alone. He wanted to be with Roberta.

They said goodnight and turned out the lights, but Roberta came up to him and kissed him with unbridled passion. Harvey responded, holding her so tight he never wanted to let go. Roberta backed away and said a little breathlessly, "Harvey, there is nothing more. I would love to crawl in bed beside you right now, but both of us have been through the heartache brought on by emotions. I'm beyond emotional tonight. I don't want us basing our happiness on a broken moment brought on by a bad day. I'd rather make that choice because it's a good day. Do you understand?" She held his arms in place around her.

Harvey said softly, "I think I both do and do not understand. I do understand I've never wanted anyone more than you. I've loved you from the minute I saw you get out of your car on the night you came to rescue Anna. My heart has laughed, cried, and been through the gambit of emotions because of the unbelievable things we've shared together in the last year. You're my person, my love, my everything as she loosened her desperate grip on him a little. "But I do choose to respect your wishes and to do whatever makes you happy. I want to spend the rest of my life with you, Roberta McEniry."

"You're a good man, Harvey Waggoner, a really good man, and I love you too," replied Roberta. She kissed him lightly one more time, then turned and walked down the hall towards her bedroom. Harvey watched her progress then smiled as she looked back at him. "Good night" they said in unison and she disappeared into her room.

Harvey stood for a while in thought. He recognized that he was hugely disappointed, but at the same time, not disappointed at all. For all his passion of the moment, he knew she was a very complex woman and had her standards set very high. He would never pressure her or try to force himself on her if only because of the horror this woman has been through in her life. He was determined to wait this out. He loved her so deeply it was almost scary, and he knew that this wait was well worth the struggle.

Harvey went to the kitchen to let Velcro out. He then made a quick turn around the house to make sure everything was secure and turned off the lights before he turned in.

When Harvey got to bed, he felt overwhelmed, and needed to pray. He hadn't had a serious cleansing talk with God in a long time. For sure, he would say bullet prayers and plead for help in certain situations, but he felt in his heart he needed a longer conversation. In the quiet of his bedroom, Harvey told God all about Roberta and his love, and their situation with Anna. He told Jesus everything! He felt a peace sweep over him. For the first time in a long time, he suddenly felt a warming wave over him that everything would be okay. He knew there was never a promise for tomorrow, but for now he felt so thankful and so grateful that he was asleep in no time. Even before he fell asleep, he felt the passion burning deep down in his groin had passed and he felt nothing but the deepest purest of loves.

• • •

The following morning, Roberta was up and coffee, muffins, and fruit were on the table by the time Harvey appeared. She had already been on the phone to make sure everything went as planned, and to get a rundown on several other areas of her level of responsibility, (which as a point of fact did not include inspections of placement of infants). She had always been one to go above and beyond her duty and liked getting her hands dirty on tough cases.

163

For the past three years or so, she had become more visible to everyone in the department as well as leaders in the state. In Roberta's mind there were still huge holes that needed to be filled to protect her kids. The most important one was a good attorney who would be available all the time (and not sleeping with his assistant). She also needed a better tracking system for each division in the state. So many things she still needed work, but having her feet on the ground with the children always gave her an uncanny level of energy and creative spirit.

It was now five days to Christmas. Roberta looked around her house and saw only a modest sprinkling of Christmas cheer. She loved Christmas but always felt guilty because there were children everywhere who never even experienced its joy.

Harvey came into the kitchen dressed in his lazy sweats and sweatshirt. He let Velcro out and immediately went to fix the dog's bowl for breakfast while Roberta was finishing her phone call. It wasn't freezing outside, just cold and wet, which was normal for this time of year if snow passed them by. He gave Roberta a side hug, then grabbed a cup of coffee and took a seat at the table.

He took his phone to check his messages, and then picked the sports section up off the table. Roberta never had much time for reading the local papers, he thought, and he'd been so busy he didn't have an idea of what was going on anywhere. Between preparing briefs for his trial, getting chased by the cartel's flunkies, and taking care of Roberta and 'her' children, he didn't have much time for anything else. He smiled at the recognition that he was content and did not really care.

She finally hung up with her call and they started eating breakfast. Before they could drift into the usual small talk, Harvey looked at her with a smile and a firm nod. Out of the blue, Harvey said, "Why don't you go into the office today and wind things up for a few days? You haven't had any time off, and neither have I. Let's hop on a plane and fly to Las Vegas. And then we'll get married." He shocked himself by saying the words, but he loved the sound of them. Roberta dropped her muffin and looked stunned.

Harvey dropped to one knee and said, "Would you marry me, Roberta McEniry? I want to marry you. I love you and you love me. This is the light of day and we're both well rested. No horrible things are going on right now. I want to marry you. Will you marry me?"

He looked at her with a huge grin spreading on his face. "I love you, girl. You fulfill my life, my wants, and my desires. As Jack Nicholson said, you make me want to make me a better man!"

CHAPTER 24

ROBERTA SAT IN SHOCK, STARING AT HARVEY LIKE HE was Santa Claus or something. She didn't feel uncomfortable with the idea of marriage, it felt right to her. *But Las Vegas? Tomorrow? Really?*

Harvey began to feel nervous, wondering if he had overplayed his hand. Roberta was still staring at him with her eyes wide open. He prodded her gently, "Roberta, what do you say?"

"What's the rush, Harvey? We haven't even slept together yet, so it's not like I'm pregnant or anything. Why the rush?" she asked again, a sheepish crossing her face.

"Okay, let me use my attorney skills here," he answered. "First, let's get the big question out of the way. Will you marry me?"

"Harvey," she answered. "I do love you more than I even understand, and yes, I will marry you."

"Okay, now we're getting somewhere," Harvey said, rubbing his hands together. "And a big 'yay' to that answer! Now let me make my case for the timing. We've both had marriages before, so we're going in with eyes wide open. Our careers are solid so we can make it together financially. We certainly don't need the whole walk down the aisle, fancy cake, and all the trimmings to prove we love each other. We've been through so much together. I don't want anyone there but you and me.

"In addition, if we go now, we could wake up together on Christmas morning as husband and wife."

He paused to take a deep breath and a sip of coffee, eying her to look for any sign that she was softening. "As for Las Vegas, it seems to be the option with the least hassle. We could go anywhere, but Vegas is fun and convenient and would give us exactly the memories we need. No one will know where we are, so we won't need any protection from law enforcement because of Mexican cartels. Besides, Vegas has the best security available. And the best part is that you won't have to take any time planning. All we have to do is show up. Las Vegas is a great place to have a wedding. They supply the flowers, the preacher, music, and even the witnesses. I'll even order our own private wedding cake to have for breakfast. I'll handle all the arrangements and we get to spend our first night in Las Vegas on a honeymoon. You have to admit, it's the perfect plan."

"You know if we're both here in town we're going to get pulled into something," he continued. "It could be anything from another child in peril to a shoot-out at the Justice of the Peace. This is the perfect time and place to do something that we have already agreed we want to do.""

Roberta sat with her mind rolling a thousand miles an hour. Despite what Harvey said, there would be a huge number of things she would need to do before she left town. She wondered if she were crazy, or maybe just crazy in love!

"Okay Counselor," she said with a smile. "You have proven your case. I think it's a great idea. Let's do it!" All her concern melted away and her heart sang with joy and happiness.

They spent the next few hours reworking their schedules from their phones and, eventually, Harvey went to shower and dress. Despite his comments, he had a ton of things to do before he left. Roberta did too. As she merrily called and changed meetings and appointments, she was surprised at herself. She was usually one to plan things, but this felt right, so right to her. She was even excited and giddy on the way to the office.

The first person she called was Kelly, her CASA friend. Kelly thought she was calling for an update report, so began to tell Roberta everything that had transpired since they saw each other. The baby had been placed back with the couple who had her since birth. They were an adoptive resource as well; the services try and place infants with potential adoptive parents where possible so a bond can develop. The infant was malnourished with rashes all over her body from dirt, dehydration, flea bites, lack of normal bathing diaper care, but she was overall healthy. She was in good hands now. The social worker seemed to have gone into turbo drive in recommending that the court return the baby to the original couple. Roberta smiled as she recognized the effect of her chat with the social worker yesterday afternoon.

"Are you done now Kelly?" Roberta asked in a lighthearted way when her friend finally took a breath of air.

"Well, yes, I guess so," the CASA shot back. "Why the hell are you so cheery this early afternoon, Miss Roberta?"

"Because I won't be "Miss Roberta" for very much longer," she squealed. "I'm getting married!"

The two celebrated together over the phone. Kelly was overwhelmed with happiness for her friend. She knew how smitten she was with this guy but had no idea they would be getting married tomorrow.

• • •

After a tedious day and evening getting things ready, both Harvey and Roberta settled in and talked on the phone for about an hour in bed. Harvey was at his place and Roberta at her place. Both were ecstatic and couldn't believe what they were doing. They were actually getting married! This would be the last night that they were in separate beds.

After having the whole day to think about it, Roberta was glad they were going through with this now. It was getting harder and harder to resist Harvey coming to bed with her, even though something had been holding her back. Maybe it was being raised in a preacher's home and the good morals she was taught that everyone should have (except her parents, of course). She felt a little sting when thinking about them, but it soon passed with the on-going excitement.

She could only imagine now how hard it must have been for Harvey to have abstained. Yet he never pushed her, never made sly or bitter comments about not sleeping together. He had been so respectful of her wishes and feelings, that somehow, she believed that God had shown her favor towards Harvey and his actions. This man had to have come directly from God. Their story was unusual from its very beginning. She felt truly blessed, thankful to be in such a beautiful relationship after everything she had already lived through with her parents and her first, bitter marriage. Her love with Harvey felt special and new. She was glad she had waited but now she can hardly hold off much longer. For tonight, it was worth it all. She rolled over smiling amazed at how excited she was for tomorrow.

They both barely slept that night, so excited about what was to come. She was up early figuring out what she wanted to wear. Harvey had been busy on the phone the day before, setting up first class flights and the honeymoon suite at Caesar's Palace. He had everything booked the chapel that was recommended by the hotel. The hotel would provide a limo and a private dinner in their room to follow. Harvey ordered the flowers, selected a few of their favorite tunes, and felt ready to venture off on his new life with his bride.

He had been worried that Gunner would be shocked and disgruntled to be left with a butt-load of work, but Gunner displayed only excitement. "Harvey, you've finally found her!" was his only response to his friend's news.

Harvey felt all was well and he was looking forward to a few days off alone with Roberta. He intended to take her to Hawaii or Fuji Islands in the spring for a real honeymoon. He didn't want to push the envelope and try to do it now. He knew how hard he had to work to get her to agree to the short trip now. She would never agree to pick up and leave for a couple of weeks. He decided to take what he could get.

CHAPTER 25

THE WEDDING WENT OFF WITHOUT A HITCH, AND BOTH Harvey and Roberta were surprised to experience such bliss the way their crazy lives had gone. It had seemed to be their pattern to get almost comfortable when something would blow up. But this was perfect.

She had chosen to wear a lovely, brilliant red jump suit that flowed like an angel's dress. It was complemented with white French cuffs, a stylish collar, and some of her nicest jewelry to make a perfect ensemble.

Harvey wore his favorite black slacks with a light blue shirt, topped with a dark suede jacket. They both looked as if they had stepped out of a magazine. Roberta's long legs and beautiful olive skin and dark flowing hair nailed the ensemble. As for Harvey, his tall and well-toned body, stellar jaw, and eyes of blue with dark hair made him look like Cary Grant. Together they were magical.

The chapel that Caesar's Palace had recommended was perfect. The owners were very nice people and the witnesses were an older couple who loved weddings almost as much as the pastor who officiated. Strangers though they were, they stood tall with bright smiles on their faces as they witnessed the happy event. The flowers, yellow and white roses, were the perfect bouquet. Harvey had selected "One Hand One Heart" from *West Side Story* as their music, moved by the image of joining the two candles into one. Neither of them could have made this moment more perfect.

Harvey had purchased a beautiful solitaire diamond ring with a matched band of solid diamonds. It was brilliant and a showstopper. Roberta had called up her Nordstrom shopper and had her bring a solid platinum wedding band for Harvey. She almost cried when she saw the rings together for the first time. They were perfect.

"By the power vested in me by God, these witnesses, and the State of Nevada, I now pronounce you husband and wife," said the jolly, old pastor. *There it is*, Harvey thought to himself, *she is my wife*, something he had been waiting for a very long time, longer it seemed than he had known her. The couple kissed and held onto each other as if they were going on a long trip. Finally, the pastor cleared his throat and tapped them on the shoulder and said, "You have blessed your marriage and honored God by the union of your commitment and marriage to each other. You are free to leave the building now. God go with you and bring you peace everlasting."

They took the hint with a big laugh all around. The newly married couple went outside where their limo and a complimentary bottle of iced champagne awaited them. If happiness were measured on a scale from 1 to 10, their happiness rate a 22!

The driver slowly drove them back to the hotel, giving them some extra special moments together. They arrived to warm greetings from the doormen who ushered them into the hotel lobby and escorted them past the entrance to the casino floor towards their suite. Heads turned and smiled at the radiant sight of Harvey, beaming with pride, and his beautiful wife on his arm.

Now the couple we retreated to a beautifully planned dinner in the Honeymoon Suite. The meal was delicious, made more so by their happiness. They ate well but barely noticed the food; they could not take their eyes off each other. Harvey thought that Roberta was more beautiful at this moment than he had ever seen her. Dinner aside, he could barely keep his hands from reaching out to grab her.

They had their shoes off, drinking champagne and looking at the view of Las Vegas out of their luxurious room when the house phone rang. Both looked a little shocked, since only a few people knew they were in Las Vegas. Roberta asked, "Were you expecting a call?" she asked with a devilish smile. "Because I've got plans for you, Harvey Waggoner."

He grinned back at her like a fifteen-year-old schoolboy in love for the first time, his heart bursting with pride and excitement. The last thing either one of them expected was a phone call.

"Maybe it's the hotel sending us something," he said as he walked over to pick up the phone. "They've been so awesome to us on such short notice."

Harvey answered the phone and recognized the voice of Pete Murdock. "Harvey," the police officer said. "I'm sorry to call, but I didn't know when the wedding was and if you were leaving after to go somewhere else on a honeymoon."

"Well, this is a surprise Pete," Harvey answered, looking at Roberta's quizzical reaction when she heard the name of the caller.

"Are you calling to congratulate us or did the cartel follow us to Las Vegas?"

Harvey was joking, but Pete was in dire earnest when he answered, "Harvey, they blew up your house. At least we believe it was them. They're playing hard ball. Have you had any contact from suspicious characters or any strange incidents occur since we last spoke?" he asked.

"We only spoke a day or two ago about my plans. I haven't had time for any incidents," Harvey groaned in frustration.

Harvey turned his back from Roberta who was diving into the newspaper and whispered in the phone to Pete, "Does Sheriff Bloom know about this too? "

"Well, yes, Harvey," Pete answered with pride. "He's taken a personal interest in this case. I'm glad for his help. After all this case is huge for our little department and the Chief is struggling with all the outside agencies keeping him out of the loop.

"You're in good hands, Harvey. The Chief has a nose for crime like a blood hound."

Roberta had joined his side, curious to hear what was happening. Harvey put his arms around her and kissed her on the head. Although he was still overwhelmed by her and their happiness, he knew he needed to pay attention here.

Pete went on to explain that there had been a huge uptick in movement by the cartel. The rumor on the street was that there was someone out there with their products and they were going to get it back one way or the other.

Harvey had not been paying enough attention over the past week or so to notice if there were comings and goings, or anybody following him. At once it hit him how much danger he and Roberta were in. He stiffened at the thought, and Roberta moved back to the couch to wait for the entire story. All she could hear was Harvey's side of the conversation and she did not know yet what was wrong.

After about fifteen minutes of conversation, Harvey finished with a promise he would check in with the police officer the next day. He hung up the phone and plopped down beside his wife, who looked at him with her eyes full of questions.

"Just one more thing for us to worry about, my sweet love," Harvey said in answer to her unspoken interrogation. "But nothing that I'm going to let get in the way of our honeymoon."

CHAPTER 26

HARVEY TOLD ROBERTA THAT THE PHONE CALL HAD been a warning about some new activity by the cartel although he told her that Pete was always a little overboard when it came to bad news. For now, Harvey kept the attack on his house a secret, not so much because he did not feel she could share the information with her, but because it was their wedding night and he wanted them to have at least this time without worry. He would assess the damage when they got home tomorrow and then tell her everything.

But right now, he thought, *I am going to make mad, passionate love to my new bride.* They had waited so long for this time between the two of them. He hoped he was not out of practice. It had been a long while since his last physical intimacy. He was not overly worried though. Somehow, an extraordinary feeling of desire was welling up inside him and it felt amazing right now!

Roberta also didn't have a thought on her mind other than loving her man. Harvey picked her up and carried her into the bedroom where the bed was already turned down and sprinkled with rose petals. *This is magical,* Roberta thought. She had not been this happy in a very long time. She had no trust in men in general, but from the moment she had met Harvey she always knew there was something very special about him.

• • •

Around 5 AM, Harvey woke up to see daylight creeping into the sky. He turned his mind away from the wonderful night that had just passed and began to plan in earnest what he was going to do. One thing he decided was to speak to Pete outside of Roberta's earshot so that he could keep her free of any bad news at least until they headed home. Harvey lay in thought as she rolled over into his arms. He didn't speak and barely breathed for fear that he might wake her ; he just held her gently. *I am the luckiest man in the world,* he thought. *There really might be something to this waiting for an intimate relationship until marriage. I guess since God made humans, He set the rules of order for the good of man. I've never felt like this in my life! This must truly be the secret of happiness like no other. So many generations, especially his, had totally missed out on this peace.*

She did not awaken, so he just lay still cherishing every moment she slept in his arms. He could not believe the feeling in his mind, body, and spirit. It was so different from anything he ever felt.

Harvey had loved Cassie too, but this was so different. He and Cassie did not wait past two dates before they hopped in the sack. Sex is one of those things that gentlemen do not speak of if they respect a woman. But somehow, he wanted to shout to all the kids growing up not to make choices that would negate an experience like he was having at this moment.

After another hour or so, Roberta stirred, and Harvey was there to wake up with her. They embraced and within moments they were again showing love for each other like never before. Their passion carried them for the next couple of hours.

Finally, sometime after eight, Harvey picked up the phone at the bedside and called for room service to order coffee, bagels, strawberries and cream, orange juice, and the Wall Street Journal. He hopped in the shower while Roberta put on her sweats and waited for room service. By the time Harvey was out of the shower, she was finishing her first cup of coffee.

"This is pretty good stuff," she said, grinning from ear to ear. He reached over and held her in his arms once more. "Well, my dear wife, pour your husband some coffee," he said teasingly.

Over breakfast, they had a wonderful time reliving every moment of their wedding. Harvey even explained his feelings, something he never did, about how wonderful the night together was for him and his new appreciation for abstaining from sex until you find the right person you want to spend your life with, as God had intended. Roberta thought about his words and some of the bible training she had as a young girl. She had always discounted everything she had learned about God since her parents had been such a grave disappointment with their infidelities God had not even been on her radar, but now she was thinking about God in deep thought. Unlike Harvey, she didn't care if anyone else discovered this secret to happiness because she was living it now and that's all that mattered.

Harvey had some activities lined up for the day. He had hired a car and a driver, since he knew he would be unable to keep his hands off Roberta long enough to drive anywhere. They were going to tour Hoover Dem and then drive to have lunch by Lake Mead. He felt a little irresponsible for not facing the latest attack right away, but in the long run Harvey felt it was the right thing to do to spend one more day together without worries. They would both face reality soon enough. That evening, they would take in a Celine Dion concert in the private section. Harvey had an old college buddy that was an "attorney to the stars" so Harvey had called him for a favor. True to his nature, the celebrity attorney not only got them front row seats, but also arranged to meet Celine after the show. Harvey knew that Celine had been one of Roberta's favorite female singers of all time.

Harvey had originally wanted to stay through Monday and return on Tuesday, but now, he needed to get home and take care of whatever was left after the explosion. He just prayed that Roberta wouldn't be too mad because he withheld this important information from her. It was not like they could do anything about it. But he put that aside for a while and just focused on being together and their newly found happiness.

When they returned to the hotel after the concert, the desk handed him two messages. One was from Pete telling Harvey to call him right away. The second call was from Dori, Roberta's assistant.

CHAPTER 27

THEY WERE LANDING IN SEATTLE WHEN HARVEY TURNED to Roberta and said, "I'm sorry you married me with so much trouble on my plate."

She gave a small laugh and kissed his nose. "If we hadn't met that dark night when you found Anna, I may never have found you," she said with tears in her eyes. "I'm not sorry at all. I love you, trouble and all and I'm thankful to be here with you. We'll get through this together. These cartel thugs are messing with the wrong attorney and the wrong social worker!"

They drove directly from the airport to Port Orchard to look at Harvey's house, or what remained of it. Harvey had asked Pete to meet them there. He needed to hear the whole story and having left Roberta out of the loop in the beginning, he wanted her to have as much knowledge as he did so she would be able to plan to look out for herself. He knew Roberta was a fighter and survivor, so he wasn't too worried about her. Just the same, he thought he should take her to the shooting range for a little target practice.

Pete arrived within minutes of the newlyweds. He congratulated them on their wedding, even stopping to briefly kiss the bride, and then he stepped aside so that Harvey and Roberta could see the damage. They stood in shock and the amount of ruin that the bombings had caused. The huge front door had been torn off and the entire façade was crumbled brick and stone. There were shards of glass everywhere so that Harvey could not imagine that there was an intact window in the place. Peering past the gaping entry, he could see the blackened remains of his lovely furniture. Roberta held his hand in hers and choked back sobs.

Pete had seen a lot of destruction in his career but had a hard time coming to terms with this explosion. He had become attached to Harvey and thought he was the bravest man he knew. He admired her as well and knew she was one tough woman. She had the tenacity of a terrier, but through Harvey, he had come to know she was the most compassionate person ever in government work. Most of the official people he had interfaced with were bureaucrats who did the minimum of their jobs, complained the most, and only cared about their paychecks. She was a different breed of cat. He hated to see two such fine people suffer.

After the initial shock had worn off, Pete said, "I have to say, you both look amazingly rested and happy, which I don't understand with all this stuff going on. I hated to have to break in your happiness with such bad news."

After Harvey nodded his acknowledgement of the sentiment, Pete returned to business. "I had the guys at the station put everything that wasn't blown up in boxes for you to go through. They're locked up at the station for safekeeping and you can come and get them anytime. Just let me know and I'll get you the key. That's not something we normally do, by the way, but we should have been watching this place more carefully, so I feel kind of responsible."

"What could you have done," Harvey asked with a shrug.

"Be more ready," Pete spat out in anger at himself. "After being quiet for all these months, there's been an uptick in activity by the group that we're watching. That said, the FBI and DEA are involved and they're not very good at sharing information. We did see some slow drive-bys by the same car but they never stopped or tried to get into the house or anything. We're assuming the drive-bys are connected with the bombing. They may have been waiting until you were in the house. I assume you had lights turned on and off with a timer, right?"

"Yes. I've always used timers when I travel. I realize the trick doesn't deter all thieves, but at least it makes them stop and figure it out," Harvey said.

"Well, in a weird way the timers helped you out here. If they hadn't seen lights, they might not have bombed the house then but waited until you really were home. The timers may have saved your life." He gave a small grunt of a chuckle, and then shook his head in shame and sorrow. "I'm really sorry Harvey. I wish I had known and could have stopped them."

"Oh, please Pete. You've gone above and beyond in this case." He patted his friend on the shoulder. "But if both Anna and her mom are dead, and the car was impounded by the cops, why are they still going after me? Do they think I somehow have their guns and drugs? Was their stuff really worth that much? I thought the driver was a small-time player."

"Yes, it was worth a lot to the small-time player, but now the cartel seems to be looking for something else. The FBI lead investigator believes it could be a file or flash drive of some kind with names on it, possibly a list of important people who are taking a cut to turn their heads the other way. That's the only thing that makes sense. This was really a small run for them to take such chances trying to get you," Pete explained. "And since we have no idea who might be involved in something like that list, if I were you, I'd be really cautious who I said what to until we have better idea of who and what are driving it all."

"Pete, promise me that you'll tell us everything that you all know or even suspect. Don't leave out any details. This is our lives we're talking about. Roberta and I are both innocent victims of a beating and robbery gone badly. We have every right to know so we can plan where we go from here," Harvey said firmly.

Pete nodded and then turned to trudge up to his car. Harvey turned to Roberta and drew her close to him. "I guess one good thing is now we know which house we're going to live in. And don't need to worry about what to keep or got rid of." She snuggled next to him, giving a little shiver that was only partly due to the cold wind.

• • •

Harvey and Roberta headed to pick up Velcro and then returned to her house. She was so excited to see them that she wagged her tail and spun in circles all the way home. Aside from Velcro's happy panting, they drove home pretty much in silence with both lost in their own thoughts. Harvey was grieving over the loss of all the things he had held onto over the years, the few things he had of Cassie's, a few things from his mother, and some private things from his old life. He felt as if someone in his life had died again.

Yet he looked around the car and realized that his most valuable and precious cargo was this woman and his dog. All his most important papers had been moved to a safety deposit box after the first attempted break-in. And the house had good insurance so he would not take too much of a financial hit on the loss. He had a lot to feel blessed about. Yet amid what should have been the happiest time of all, everything was in confusion and jeopardy. At a time when a newlywed couple should be making plans for their future, they would need to figure out how to stay safe and alive.

As they were pulling into the garage remembering they needed to pull down the Christmas decorations, Harvey's cell phone rang. He picked up to look at the number and it said, "Restricted." That piqued Harvey's curiosity enough to answer the phone, but the caller hung up without saying anything. The unlogged call disturbed him.

Roberta asked, "Was that your office checking in on you?"

"No, actually it was a hang-up call. Not a lot of people have this cell number, so it's a little weird that I would get a hang up," he said.

"Maybe someone accidentally dialed the wrong number, Harvey. Don't make this more than it is," she said.

"I'm not trying to, but my radar is pretty sensitive right now."

They unloaded the car and agreed to spend the evening catching up. Harvey fed Velcro and sat down with a glass of wine, handing one to his beautiful new wife. As they settled in, with laptops open and surrounded by their sundry files, Roberta's phone rang again.

CHAPTER 28

THE CALL THAT ROBERTA RECEIVED FROM HER ASSIStant in Las Vegas was about a case that Dori knew was important enough to call about night or day. A ten-year-old boy, Nicky, had been in and out of care since he was born. Roberta had been involved in many steps along the way, so she knew the 'little guy' just wanted to be a part of a family and to have someone love him all the time.

The boy had been sexually and physically abused by his mother's boyfriends. There were no grandparents in the picture; the maternal grandparents were dead and the paternal grandparents either could not be found or did not want to be involved. No aunts, uncles, or cousins had been located except for the mother's brother who was in prison in Florida serving back-to-back life sentences. As hard as it was to bear, darling Nicky had no one at all in his corner. He was also a handful. His case had been transferred to three different social workers and two different CASAs and he had lived in six foster homes.

With no consistent adult presence throughout his time with CPS, there was nothing constant in his life but loneliness and grief.

Of course, he developed the attitude that many unwanted children do that sets them on the wrong road for life. At ten years old, the attitude was growing into his personality and his constant irreverent behavior made this case one of the toughest Roberta had dealt with in years.

Now the child had tried to take his own life. Roberta knew she had to do something. The foster care he was in was okay, but they had several kids of their own, all older than Nicky. They didn't want their own kids influenced by this young boy. Roberta decided she would pay Nicky a visit on her way into the office in the morning.

Harvey went back to work in a sweat knowing he had a lot hanging over his head. The trial was just winding down to its last few days; Gunner had done an amazing job representing their client and had even uncovered fraud on the opposing side. With the case going their way, Harvey suggested that Gunner do the close. While that was Harvey's specialty (giving a lot of credit to Cassie and the strategies he learned from her), he felt that Gunner was due for another big win. Oddly, the case was not all that important to Harvey. He had his wife and was wrapped up in finding a pathway for their lives, and of course he had the rotten cartel trying to kill him for information he did not even have. His level of enthusiasm for representing big organizations was not as high on the to-do list as before.

He had heard a lot of the cases Roberta was involved with and his heart was touched by all of them. His original intent in studying law had been to be a person that helps kids in transition and in need. Now he was hearing all the stories and he wanted to jump in and represent these kids against not only their incompetent parents, but also against a system that was antiquated, corrupt, and out of sync with the needs of children, a system that had lost its way. Regardless of the ever-increasing numbers of failures: suicides, gun violence threats, and even murders Among children in the system, there were no state or municipal leaders that even breathed the words "Child Protective Services" leaving that up to a nebulous Government that did not care or share.

Kids, especially those in foster care, are targets for national and international sex trafficking rings. Children would be stolen out of back yards, from malls, churches, streets, and especially on-line through Tick-Toc and other social media platforms. Harvey had never worked in politics, or the government for that matter, but it disgusted that the system had not had any attention in more than fifty years. He became physically ill when he thought about these children who society had failed.

For now, he would try and wrap up his pending cases and maybe decide to do something entirely different. To Harvey, things were different now. He had no idea how much he could love a woman again, not just because she was beautiful, sexy, silly smart, and compassionate, but because he respected her as much as he loved her. Through her example, he could tell he no longer had the compassion for his job that he might have had once, if ever.

Harvey's assistant buzzed him to say that Roberta McEniry was on line two. He smiled and replied, "Its Roberta McEniry Waggoner now, thank you."

"Hey, how's the madness going in your corner?" he said with a lift in his voice when she was on the line.

"Are you really busy, Harvey, or can I borrow you for about an hour?" Roberta asked with a stressed voice.

Harvey was about to make the comment that he was always more than available to ravage her body, but he sensed the urgency in her voice and simply asked what she needed.

"I have a situation. Would you mind coming to pick me up and go with me on a call? I would have one of the other men here to go with me, but honestly, I don't trust any of the ones who are here," she replied.

"Of course," he said instantly, proud to be included in her trust. "I'll pick you up at the south side entrance."

Within minutes he was at the door and Roberta hopped into the car. Harvey would have said some sweet nothing to her, but he could see how tense and focused she was, lacking even the gorgeous smile with which she usually greeted him. Harvey had seen her like this before, usually during a case in which something was going sideways. He decided to be quiet and just drive.

CHAPTER 29

"I JUST GOT A CALL FROM THE DEA WHO IS WORKING on a sting operation in Fife," Roberta explained. "There's a hotel that we know of which is commonly used for holding sex-trafficking victims to transfer either to the airport or across the border to Mexico. The victims are girls and boys of all ages between 5 and 17. Almost always these children have been abducted or tricked into coming by the pedophiles and sex traffickers."

"There are many, thousands of pedophiles, mostly men, living in the suburbs of our community right next door to Johnny-do-good's families. You know, church goers, involved in the PTA, or sports coaches who are paid by the cartel, although they might not know it's the cartel, to find the kids and pass on their names. The cartels take it from there…if you know what I mean. If one of these 'scouts' gives a name, a description, and some small piece of knowledge about a kid that has a poor self-image, or maybe living in harm's way, or especially a foster child, they get paid a huge amount of money for a completed transaction. There are different levels; different jobs from introducing kids to drugs and so on."

Harvey sat still and listened in earnest to this woman who had probably experienced everything she is talking about in the smallest of detail. Harvey thought, *how does she do this job without suspecting or hating everyone?* Not for the first time, he recognized that she was an amazing woman.

"There are women involved too, don't let me make you think it's all men," she continued. "They're paid based on whether they are asked to sample products or to provide out personal information about the kids. You see, some of the politicians, celebrities, rich Arabs, and just the lowest scum of the earth people demand product that isn't 'soiled' or 'used'. The product I'm speaking of is a child's body. They like to be the first to penetrate their buy. Some deals are made for just sheer pleasure, and some for profit as the buyers move kids internationally to the highest bidder. Many times, there are even connections to high-ranking officials in the FBI, CIA and the Military."

Harvey listened intently, feeling sicker in his stomach hearing about the situation. The feeling was intensified by the passion Roberta showed for helping these kids. He kept visualizing the horror on Anna's face, and other faces he had seen and how that fear must be magnified when a grown man stoops down to enter their young body. He rolled down the window a little to breathe the cold, fresh air.

Roberta noticed what he was going through and quickly apologized for the colorful descriptions. She sometimes has so much anger built up she had to say it out loud to keep from killing someone!

"Harvey I'm sorry to be so blunt," she said with compassion.

"Oh no," said Harvey holding his hand up to her. "I need to hear this. If I'm going to be your support, I need to know exactly what I'm dealing with. We all hear stories about this madness, but we usually don't learn the foul details. Out of sight, out of mind, right? After all, it's happening to someone else's kid." Harvey swallowed the lump of anger that had formed in his throat. "Please, I owe you an apology for not understanding the horrific reality of these children. Please go on. I want to hear it all."

"For now," Roberta said gently, "let's stay focused on the case that's in front of us. It doesn't get much worse in a lot of ways than what you're about to see."

She went on to explain that during a recent raid, DEA confiscated a large white utility van full of children who had been locked in for days. They had been left some water and a few blankets, but no food and nowhere to go to the bathroom. The captors threatened that if the children yelled, screamed, or cried, they would know and kill their parents, sisters, brothers. And even any dogs or cats in the family. The threats had worked well. The children cowered in the van and never made a noise.

Four children were rescued during the actual sting exchange operation, but the agents only found the van parked behind a nearby gas station when a little six-year-old girl wanted to know what had happened to her sister. She told them all about the van and the threats. Fourteen other children were stuffed in that van. The agents could smell it before they even arrived.

Roberta took a deep breath and let it out as a weary sigh. "I've made arrangements for a nearby hotel to make several rooms available to clean up the kids. I've called in my most trusted team of social workers and health care workers to assist with getting evidence from these children and provide food and clothing from our office's emergency closet. At the same time, we're trying to treat each one of them with love and compassion and to offer whatever support they need. We want to get this entire group processed before we notify the parents of those children who have them. Those kids will be brought to another hotel and wait until the FBI can notify their families. For the children without families, we'll have social workers standing by with the child's file in hand to help place them.

"One of the things the healthcare staff will be doing is trying to collect verifiable evidence that will hold up in a court of law. We have learned half of our struggle is not having accurate evidence of abuse collected properly at that moment of discovery."

"I'm speechless," Harvey said. "I'm just speechless."

"I haven't told you about this until now because I never really thought I'd need to. This was my world, and I was protecting the kids and my department, trying to stay within protocol. But we're critically short-handed now, like on the other occasions where you helped me out. I had a judge process an emergency appointment for you to act in the best behalf of these children, under the supervision of a senior supervisor, and to be on site at a scene." She reached into her briefcase pulling out a badge with his name on it.

"Since you are an attorney at the bar in Washington State and are in good standing with your law firm and the courts, the appointment was approved. I hope you don't mind, Harvey," she said sheepishly.

"Are you kidding me?" Harvey said proudly. 'Of course, I don't mind. It's my honor to help these kids and my privilege to stand by my incredible wife and do whatever I need to do."

"Well," Roberta said, "I'm really glad you feel that way because I have an assignment for you already. There's a 10-month-old baby girl that was abducted with her older sister who was watching her while her mom was in the dressing room. I'm going to need you to be her guardian throughout this investigation. Can you do that? Someone will be there in the room helping you." She looked into his eyes. "The baby is probably pretty sick. There may not be much to do but hold her. The kids said they had to hold their hands over her mouth so hard to keep her quiet, that she "went to sleep" several times and then became too weak to cry."

CHAPTER 30

WHEN THEY ARRIVED AT THE SCENE, IT SEEMED LIKE a chaotic mess. People were rushing back and forth, with children being led by caring adults to the various areas for help. Everyone looked shocked and terrified, as if they had just seen Satan.

Roberta pointed towards one of the rooms. "That's where the baby is. The officer and the care worker will leave when you get there, since they have to do other things. Just do the best you can do to comfort the girl. I know you'll do great."

She gave him an encouraging kiss and Harvey jumped out of the car, sprinting across the parking lot to the room she had indicated. He could smell the odor the minute he entered the room. The police office and social worker both had masks on. They checked Harvey's badge and gave him a nod as they flew out of the door to their other duties.

The infant was lying almost lifeless on the room's small bed, her clothes filthy with grim and waste. Harvey reached down and scooped up this priceless life in his arms, then found a chair to begin rocking and singing softly. Harvey had been raised in a 'singing church' so he knew how to sing with a sweet, baritone voice. He began singing some of the old hymns that he loved, starting with "Jesus Loves Me."

After his first song, he noticed that there was a sack lying on the dresser that had fresh blankets and clothes. He figured that it had been brought in by the social workers or the police. Holding the baby in his arms he went into the bathroom and picked up a clean towel off the rack. He soaked it in warm water and then returned to the bed and began unfolding the stinky blanket. Digging in the sack he found a clean diaper and a fresh change of clothes and socks.

Once Harvey had finished washing the child, he dressed her and brought her back to the chair, stopping to turn the thermostat way up since it was freezing in the room. He sat down again and continued with his soft singing, holding her ever so gently and securely in her warm, clean wrapping. With time. She opened her eyes and looked completely into his soul. His entire body melted under her gaze as she began moving ever so slightly. Harvey gave her room to squirm a little but still held her firmly in his arms.

As if on cue, another social worker flew into the room with a bottle full of white liquid, whether formula or milk Harvey did not know. She gave a distressed smile and asked him to try and get the girl to eat, but not to force the food if she was not ready. Before Harvey could answer, the woman had disappeared back out of the door.

Harvey took the bottle and gently put it to her lips while a tiny bit of milk spilled down her cheek. She quickly licked her lips and began screaming for the bottle. Her screams reminded him of Anna's at the side of the road that night he would never forget. He quickly shook off the memory and focused on how to feed this starving baby.

She only drank for a few minutes and nodded off, but Harvey could feel a difference in her relaxed sleep. She obviously felt safe now.

Harvey did not know how long he sat there, singing and listening to all the madness going on outside his closed door: children crying and wailing, social workers sobbing, and even hardened policemen shaken by the enormity of the rescue effort. After a while, the noise and chaos seemed to be quieting down.

It was then a familiar figure passed outside the room. Harvey as he could have sworn it was Sheriff Bloom. He hopped up from his chair, holding the baby tight, and looked down the hallway in both directions. He saw nothing and scolded himself for always seeing something that wasn't there. Nevertheless, he rewarded himself with a pat on the back; he had been through a lot of trauma the past several months and he seemed to be on constant alert, even if he did not know why.

He took his seat with the baby snuggled close to him and reminded himself this was not about him. This was about the kids.

Harvey zoned out only to have the spell broken by the sound of his wife's voice outside. Roberta stuck her head through the door, smiled, and walked over to Harvey to give him a kiss on the forehead.

"Let's face it my dear," she said, surveying the peaceful scene. "You just have a way with battered and abused children!".

"Anyway, I wanted you to know that you're off the hook. A social worker has arrived to take this baby and her sister back to their parents. The parents will take the children to a trauma hospital where they'll be looked over with a fine-tooth comb. Hopefully then their ordeal will be over, and they can finally go home." Roberta looked exhausted but proud. She loved taking stolen and broken children back to a loving home. Moments like this made all the bad days worth the fight.

Even though Harvey was reluctant to let her go, transferring the baby did not wake her up. *That must be a good sign*, he thought. With Anna, anyone touching her brought on more screams even when she calmed down. *Yes, this is really good. This child has parents that love her and are waiting to keep her safe again.*

When the social worker had gone off to the other hotel site, Roberta checked in with the rest of the crew and confirmed that the processing was just about done for the day. She looked around at the slowing trickle of activity and gave a small nod.

With the last of the children heading to safety, Harvey and Roberta walked arm in arm back to their car. She looked at him with love and admiration, knowing that there was no one else like her Harvey who would do anything for children. She could always count on him to do and say the right things.

"You worried me a little back there," Roberta said as Harvey looked at her quizzically. "I wondered for a minute if we were going to have a replay of what happened with Anna. You handed off the baby without any fuss this time. I am so proud of you. Your first DEA sting operation! Way to go Harvey. Perfectly orchestrated."

He smiled slightly and shrugged his shoulders but was very proud of himself and his beautiful wife. "I imagined that she was headed to be with her parents, and it was so much easier. I'd love to know how she does." Only now did he allow himself to flash back to that night with Anna and how the fentanyl was already taking over her mind and body.

"What about drugs? What about fentanyl?" Harvey asked with panic in his tone.

"What do you mean about fentanyl?" She looked at him in horror. "Did you see any fentanyl?"

"No, I didn't see any. I just remember how it took a while for the fentanyl to eventually kill Anna."

Roberta softened into a soothing tone. "The dogs had already sniffed every inch of that trailer and the hotel before we got there and found no evidence of fentanyl. If there had been fentanyl present, the DEA and FBI agents would have been in hazmat suits. That said, the captors might have had drugs in their possession, but so far the children have been cleared of any exposure."

Harvey's breathing became easier, although he knew he would have to live with the aftershocks of what he had just witnessed for a long time.

• • •

That evening, they slouched down on the couch, each thinking their own private thoughts about the last 72 hours. The fire was going, and Velcro lay in-between them fast asleep. Harvey decided to tell Roberta how he really felt.

"You want to do what?" Roberta shouted, rising from the couch and waking Velcro. "You want to quit your seven-figure corporate attorney job and represent abused children?"

He looked at her like a child caught with his finger in the peanut butter jar. "I thought… well, I really want to… er, is that okay?" he stammered sheepishly.

She gave him a big kiss and then fell back into her seat on the couch smiling like a spoiled child. "It's about freakin' time," she said.

CHAPTER 31

A FTER A LONG NIGHT OF DISCUSSION, THEY WENT TO bed in each other's arms, thanking God for all the blessings He had given them in bringing them together. Harvey was certain, more certain than Roberta that the union of their marriage had been planned all along. Harvey was thankful he followed through on moving from New York, and for taking the path that led him to Anna and, through her, to Roberta. They still had the cartel issue to deal with since they had just blown-up Harvey's house, but he was grateful for every moment he had with Roberta.

Everyone at his law firm in Seattle was floored by Harvey's decision to leave the firm, everyone but Gunner that is. His best buddy had already exposed his belly to him about his love for working with these kids. He knew Harvey's past, his lifelong desire to help other children, and how Harvey had wanted to do this since he was out of law school. Even though Cassie had been the wrong woman to marry for Harvey to fulfill his dreams, he never held that against his beloved first wife, but he knew one day he'd find the right opportunity.

With the firm's understanding, if not actual blessing, Harvey set up his own law practice and inadvertently brought over a couple of friends from his old employer. He made it known loud and clear that they could have all the clients they wanted, but first and foremost they each must take a minimum of two cases a year, pro bono, for children in need.

The spring of that year, Harvey started the firm officially and had already locked in several high-profile clients. Harvey's practice was to take second chair for most of the corporate clients so that he was always available and involved in helping the children. Nevertheless, his corporate practice in law had teeth. Harvey was far too good a lawyer for it to go otherwise and he did not want to waste all those years of experience.

Roberta made sure he knew about all the difficult and hard to manage cases so these children would get a fair shot. It didn't take long for Harvey's reputation to grow with CPS and the courts. Even the judges figured out they needed to make sure their ducks were in a row when he came to their courtroom. He wasn't one for long delays and he wasn't very good at accepting complacent judges that were more interested in their tee time than in the children who came before their bench.

There had been no issues for months with the cartel and their shenanigans. Even Officer Pete was surprised how after the bombing in December, there was "all quiet" on the home front. Harvey was not complacent enough to accept any of this as good news. He knew the cartel would not walk away until things were finished. They had made too big of a fuss about Harvey already and they did not want to be viewed as 'soft'. He kept his radar on high alert.

A year passed and Harvey's firm was doing awesome. Not only had they become the movers and shakers in corporate defense, but Harvey and several of his attorneys had become well known in the Juvenile Courts. His outcome on almost every one of his cases was in the "best interest of the children," not the system or the parents. Even though kids needed to be with relatives, the department was challenged to look under every nook and cranny to discover truth about these children's issues.

The courts used to have 'three strikes out', a motion put in place by the judge who started Drug Court. But the liberals had worked to eliminate that process, making the judges' jobs easier since children were placed back in the same conditions, many times with drug parents. Harvey had a personal goal to bring back a system that worked, with everyone being seen by the judge every thirty days just as in the "three strike you're out" system. This held the caregivers accountable. If they messed up, they went to jail for 30 days. In the current Social Service system, the time of review was supposed to be ninety days at best. Most of the time, that date fell through the cracks, sometimes as long as 120 days or more, leaving the children in all kinds of danger from parents that were supposed to be following a plan, but didn't. Onerous as it was, the thirty-day plan was a great system that worked for a long time.

Once parents missed anything such as a urine test, didn't show up for a visit, missed at work, or were caught drinking or doing drugs, they were placed in jail for 30 days. The qualifiers of the 30 days were all created for each case. With the help of the then CASA (Court Appointed Special Advocate) program, this process worked really well. The CASAs were the eyes and ears for the judge. Their reports were read first, even ahead of the social workers. CASAs were volunteers who were there for one reason. Their only objective as unpaid "voices of the child in court" was to help abused and abandoned children. CASAs were to be consistent people in their lives, required to make visits and meet the parents regularly and file a written report. Many times, they were the ones who could express the wishes of the child, a point of view that was often overlooked.

Harvey recalled one CASA asking the judge if the child could address the court. The little boy was seven years old and had been in and out of the system his entire life. His words allowed not only the judge but also the mom who could not stay clean and sober through one full cycle most of this kid's life to understand what he was going through.

The judge called him to the witness chair and went through the appropriate oath, then he asked the young boy what he had to say. Without hesitation he looked the judge square in the eyes and said, "Mr. Judge, I love my mother. I love her more than anything in the world. But she is sick, very sick, and has been sick for a long time."

He paused to wipe his nose with his shirt, and then looked out at the CASA for an encouraging nod and smile. "Mr. Judge," he continued. "I want to be with my mama in a bad way. I miss her every day and every night. But I want my mama to be healthy. Can you help me?"

A tear was streaming down the boy's cheek, and he was not alone. There wasn't a dry eye in the court room. Even the judge sniffed back a sob. His mother broke down and cried out loud, so the child jumped out of his seat and went to his mother's side to comfort her. "See Mr. Judge? See what I'm talking about? She is sick, very sick. Help her please, Mr. Judge."

The CASA went over and gently took the child to his seat at the table where she was sitting with the social worker. The judge was almost speechless. He called the mother out by name. "Look at me. Up here, look at me," he said sternly. The mother finally raised her head from the table with her bloodshot eyes and running nose.

"This child is broken-hearted," the judge said. "He cries himself to sleep every night worrying about his mother. He's wondering if she is safe, wondering if she is still 'sick'.

"It's time you got your act together. If not, only you will be responsible for letting your child down. It's time for action, now. You've got thirty days to prove that you can be a mother to me and this court... starting now."

Harvey learned a great deal through this experience. He could not have been prouder of the child and the judge. The boy's speech and the judge's response produced wonderful results. The mom did get better to the point that the court allowed her son to stay with her under house rules: surprise visits all the time and keeping in touch daily with the social worker. By now, the mother was almost six months clean and was on the way to getting her son back permanently.

Roberta was head of the entire state operation now and was on the Board of Advisors for the National CPS Program, although she continued to handle cases in the field because that was where she felt most needed and where she could keep her hand on the pulse of trends affecting our children.

She had been able, with Harvey's help, to change policies and procedures that were casting a wider net on parents' shadow activities. More children were sent home with their parents only after the parents had earned the respect of the courts and had locked down parenting skills in their lives. Those who chose to think they could still hide behaviors from the system were easily discovered through the new procedures and laws. Now the emphasis was focused on finding qualified foster parents and adoptive resources.

It helped that Roberta had close friends who had long experience of being CASAs. They were her boots on the ground feeding information to anyone who would listen about ideas and protocols that would better protect and serve children. They could also provide information about the continued surge in sex trafficking by the cartels in Mexico. The problem was running rampant, and the FBI and DEA were swamped.

CHAPTER 32

I N EARLY AUTUMN, ROBERTA WAS OUT IN HER BACK-yard checking on the special flowers which she loved. Their family had grown by one; Harvey went to the dog shelter and picked up a little boxer whose owners had just given up and presented him to Roberta for her birthday.

They named the dog Borax which meant 'keeper'. Roberta loved this dog and Velcro had taken him under her wings knowing she had been a shelter dog too. Somehow animals seem to know this. Velcro, who was normally stingy with her mom and dad, shared everything with Borax. She would give up her lap time with her dad and even share her food and toys.

As Roberta was moving around in the flower beds, she heard a ticking noise. Curious, she started using her sheers to dig around the flowers until she uncovered a box. She immediately grabbed Borax and called Velcro to get in the car. She grabbed her keys and phone, breathing heavily as she reached the car. The garage door seemed to take forever to open as she called Harvey.

On his end of the line, Harvey smiled when he saw Roberta's caller ID. *This is so sweet*, he thought. *She's calling me even before I get home.*

"Hey sweet pea, you got any good ideas for tonight?" he said with a smile.

His smile was wiped out by the panic in her voice. "Harvey, I think there's a bomb in the backyard. I picked up the dogs and ran to my car. Should I call 9-1-1?"

Harvey snapped alert. "Yes, call now, then call me back. Get out of there and park far away from the house. I'll be right there." Fortunately, Harvey's new office was in Gig Harbor, making it easy for him get home.

Roberta called the police, who responded immediately. Within a few minutes, although it seemed longer to her, the police arrived along with a fire truck and ambulance. The bomb squad had been put on alert and was waiting for confirmation before heading to Gig Harbor.

"Where exactly is the ticking box?" the responding policeman politely asked her. "And why would you expect a bomb?" She could tell from his tone that he thought she might be some crazy lady having wine time too early, but he knew that bombs were nothing to be taken lightly.

Roberta explained to the officer they had been threatened by the cartel and had one house blown up already. She mentioned Pete by name as well as the DEA and the FBI working on their case. The Officer's attention instantly changed, and he ordered the bomb squad to come.

About the same time Harvey was speeding down the street and squealing his brakes to a stop. He had called Pete on the way home and told him. Pete said he was on his way and that he would notify the FBI agents still on the case.

The police went to the doors of both next-door neighbors and asked them to come outside in the street behind cover until the bomb threat was neutralized. By this time the entire neighborhood was on their front lawns wondering what was going on. Roberta thought to herself, *Oh great, now everyone will know and keep their distance. So much for privacy.*

After a half hour or so, the Bomb Squad van pulled close to the police cars. Men jumped out of the van and began gearing up. A small robot with a collecting box in front was mobilized.

Pete arrived flashing his badge to get where the action was taking place. He announced who he was and confirmed Roberta's story about their home being bombed a couple of years ago. He told the lead police officer that they had assumed the cartel had moved on but evidently, they had not.

Roberta returned to the car to check on the dogs. Velcro was calm once she saw Harvey, but Borax was a mess. Velcro was doing her best to calm him down. Roberta tried to give them reassurance but kept them in the car for their protection. Borax was none too happy although Velcro seemed to understand.

It had been a long time since Roberta saw such deep concern on Harvey's face, so she was truly worried. Her main concern up until then was that she had overreacted. But Harvey had frequently warned her to stay alert. He knew that the cartel would never back down, if only to maintain their reputation.

Harvey was really concerned this time, not so much for their immediate safety, but for the future. They would need to move again and even then, he knew the cartel would track them down. He resolved not to think about that now. Instead, he would focus on this moment then he and Pete would get together and plan.

The robot slowly made its way through the side gate to the backyard. It seemed to already know the place where Roberta had seen the box. They had her tell repeatedly where the box was and what was around it. The bomb squad was watching the camera waiting for further instructions while the robot technician worked the levers to make it move.

"It sure looks and sounds like a bomb," said the tech running the device and listening with earphones. The robot came back to the edge of the gate and picked up a small steel box then returned to the bomb. The arm picked up the package ever so gently and placed it in the steel box, closing the lid. As soon as the lid was closed, it started toward the side gate. The robot had just reached the side of the house next to the garage when the package exploded. The agent operating the robot cried out, "Holy crap! I'm not sure we can get another one of these in this year's budget." The agents around him all shook their heads in agreement and went to gather the pieces.

The agent running the robot whispered something to the lead detective and walked off. The officer came over to Roberta and Harvey and said, "It looks like there was a timer on this thing. We can't tell when it was set to go off since so much of the machinery has been destroyed, but we'll get back to you when we find out more." He smiled and walked away to call in the firemen and hoses.

"Miss Roberta, it looks like you were right," admitted the first responding police officer. "Thank goodness you called. You are one smart lady for spotting that device but not touching it. As you witnessed, sometimes even the smallest movement can make it go off."

CHAPTER 33

SINCE THERE WAS A HOLE IN THEIR BEDROOM WALL, they decided to get a room at a hotel nearby. They went into the house with officers at their side to get their things together, along with dogs' beds and food. A crew was sent in to board up the hole. The neighbors were relieved but could not believe what they had just seen.

By the time Roberta and Harvey headed back to the car, most of the officials had loaded up and taken off. Velcro was standing up in the car, but Borax was fast asleep. Velcro had stood at alert the entire time; she had been through this before and again was concerned for her master. The dog had tears in her eyes and looked so sad that Harvey stuck his head in the door and said some calming words. He knew how traumatic all this had been for her – for all of them.

Roberta was still in shock. She had wanted to believe that this Chapter of their life had been over, but the bombing proved painfully that it was not.

Harvey could see the pain in her eyes. "I'm sorry, Roberta," he said in the same calming and confident voice that he had used to lull Velcro. "I had hoped we were done with this. But we're not. Pete is going to the FBI now to find out any new information and we're going to meet up in the morning. You can go to work tomorrow or not. That's your call. If we need other things there will be an officer to accompany us to the house so don't worry about that. I'll spend tomorrow looking for a place for us to live for a few months until we decide what to do. We don't need to decide anything at this moment. We'll get through this fine."

He was trying to work out in his head how he was going to do all this. He had a very important case coming up on Friday he could not miss. Harvey decided that a case discussion just might be the thing to help Roberta over the hump, so he told her the details. "I'm due in court on the Kendall case on Friday. This little girl needs to find out if her parents are for real or not, although my personal opinion is that the evidence shows they're still using and that her mom is still hooking in the streets." Harvey was attached to this case since it was one of the first, he had taken on with his new firm and it had already been in the system for two years.

The little Kendall girl was two-and-a-half years old and more than adorable. Her mom had delivered her then left her at the hospital to get on another high. Social Services didn't find her for almost three months. She showed up in jail and suddenly decided to become a mom.

Since then, she and baby daddy got together again and wanted the baby back. The system gave her back even though they knew the parents were not clean and sober long enough to measure. but the lack of spaces to keep babies and exhausted, overworked social workers kept pushing for reconciliation. That led to the abandonment of this infant; the parents left the baby alone in an abandoned house for two nights while they were out on a high. The case was dragged back to court where the child became the pawn. The child showed signs of gross neglect even during planned visits with CPS. What are these parents thinking, anyway? It was a disgusting case of everything gone wrong for this child and Harvey had had enough.

Harvey repeatedly visited the parents, and they were always a little mentally unstable. This was one of those cases where the parents never performed but somehow convinced the social worker and courts they were trying and doing well. They said the "system" was against them, bringing all kinds of lies and accusations.

• • •

Roberta and Harvey had to drive to Tacoma to get a room. They agreed to get a suite with a kitchenette so they could use a microwave and a toaster. And of course, it needed to have a coffee pot. Neither of them slept very well that night. Nor did the dogs. They might have slept better had they known that Pete had put a tail on them to watch over their every move for protection. After all, as Pete told Harvey in private at the site of the bomb, there was no way to predict when or what the cartel's next move might be. But they both agreed there would be a next move.

Harvey searched the internet and found a vacation rental in Gig Harbor that he thought would be perfect while waiting for the next move. He called the owner and offered him a lucrative longer term monthly lease. When the owner discovered that Harvey was a prominent attorney and represented foster kids on top of that, he agreed to a six-month rental. The house was on the waterfront west side of Gig Harbor giving them an amazing view. It was furnished and a place of beauty. Fortunately, it was available immediately, having just been cleaned for the next guest. The rental fee was high, but Harvey didn't even flinch and asked to take the property beginning the next day. He had a little persuading to do with regard to the dogs. Harvey knew that the owner would have no concern after meeting Velcro but Borax was another story. A large pet deposit smoothed the way and the contract was secured.

After putting what was left at Roberta's house into storage, Roberta and Harvey stayed a couple of nights in the hotel suite and then went to stock up and get settled into their new home. Roberta loved the house and the view, as well as the privacy of it all. She wondered if they might sell. *With an updated makeover*, she thought, *this would be a killer place to come home to.*

• • •

The day before Christmas Eve, Harvey and Roberta were sitting on the couch with the dogs and just thanking God for bringing them this far. The cartel had gone silent again for almost three months, which disturbed Harvey more than he let on. He and Pete stayed in regular contact even if it was just a brief meeting for coffee. Both thought there was more to be revealed about all of this. Pete knew more than he shared with Harvey, partly for his friend's own good but mostly because he would lose his job and jeopardize this case if he shared all the facts. Nevertheless, he kept Harvey as updated as possible and always reassured that the case was active and that he personally would not let go of until they found answers.

Sipping on their wine and eating crackers and cheese, enjoying each other's company, Roberta's phone rang. She had always left strict instructions to let her know of any potential child that had fallen through the system and reappeared. She was not able to step in as often as she liked because her job was huge now. Being the state leader gave her pause every morning when she woke up. But the least she could do was keep a hand on the pulse of the lost children. She would always find time to listen and investigate to ensure that case got handled quickly. She even had her own investigators. Her fear was that she might lose the deep passion that ran through her veins if she did not know the 'boots on the ground' stories.

Roberta was on the phone for a while and came back to the couch with a very concerned look on her face.

"I know that look," said Harvey pulling her down to the couch. "What happened now?"

"How would you like to take a quick visit with me to the hospital in Tacoma?" she asked, giving him a quick kiss and standing back on her feet. "I have to go check out an important case and I'd love your company" When he shrugged his shoulders and stood up himself, she smiled at him and said, "I'll give you the scoop on the way. Don't forget your badge."

They gave Velcro and Borax their supper and treats, then turned on the TV because Borax liked watching dog food commercials, then they carefully locked up the house. As they headed across the bridge to the hospital, Roberta explained that the child was four days old, and the social worker had quit without warning. A back-up case worker was too overwhelmed with urgent cases and never got to the hospital. Even the supervisor was unavailable, recovering from a bad case of the 'flu and not allowed into the hospital's neonatal department.

The report on the case stated that the mom had sat out in front of the hospital in full labor and consumed a six pack of beer. Her blood work showed she was positive for cocaine and meth. She finally was brought into Emergency with help from the parking lot attendants, but she delivered the baby and never wanted to see it. Within six hours the mother had disappeared from the hospital after stating to the hospital social worker she wanted nothing to do with the child.

The file showed this was her sixth baby and she had not parented any of them. The baby daddy was unknown. No family showed up in any of the research when she lost custody of all her children. There was one other little girl aged four, who would be the baby's step-sister, as well as a couple of half-siblings between the ages of 6-16 that were still in the system. They were children who had fallen through the cracks and were still circling the system from foster care to foster care.

Now this baby was in trouble. She was on a ventilator and tested positive for all the substances her mother had consumed. The likelihood of the baby surviving was slim.

All these signs struck a chord with Roberta, and she told the supervisor who made her aware of the case that she would check in on the baby tonight, giving time to secure another social worker.

As Roberta and Harvey stood in the neonatal unit dressed in matching masks and paper surgical gowns, they peered into the plastic box to see life it was sustaining, the tiny 2.1-pound baby girl fighting for her life. Tubes came out of every place in her body and nurses checked in on her every 15 minutes or so.

Tears were streaming down Harvey's face, and he looked at a sobbing Roberta and said, "This little human has no one in this entire world that loves her." They both stood in silence for a long time watching this baby struggle.

Harvey began praying out loud, "Dear Jesus, this child has no one but you to love and care for her. I ask that you keep her safe and send someone to love her with everything they can possibly offer. Send the right, perfect person to care for this child. She is so innocent," he prayed. "I love this child, dear God, with all my heart. Please allow that love and your love to warm her body and keep her spirit fighting."

When he opened his eyes, Roberta was weeping. She told Harvey she loved him and buried her face in his chest. She loved his heart. She loved that he loved her and loved this baby. She had never been as proud of him for praying at the perfect time. He always told her God would show up exactly when you needed Him, and He certainly did then.

They each took a seat, Harvey in a wooden rocker and Roberta in a cushioned chair. She was lost in her thoughts of God and the tender heart she had developed for Him. She was amazed at herself since she had always been estranged from her Heavenly Father. She wasn't sure why her disdain for her earthly father had lasted so long, but she was still holding a grudge against both her parents. Now finally she knew that her relationship with God was not about her or them. Right now, it was about the child.

The nurse entered the room and broke the silent moment. She was a sweet woman full of love. Seeing the tear-stained eyes of the two visitors, she looked at Harvey and said, "Mr. Waggoner, would you like to hold her a minute? She's never been held by anyone but us nurses, and we only have a minute or so to love her when we can find the time."

Harvey's sadness turned into an overwhelming care of concern. He told her he would love to hold the child.

"Alright, then," said the nurse. "For just a few minutes since I have a full house tonight. But I know she would love to feel the warmth of someone who cares."

Ever so gently, she caressed the baby out of her warming box so as not to pull out any wires. She instructed Harvey to pull his rocker right up to the baby's plastic bed and she would bring the girl over. Harvey could hardly breathe. He'd never held such a tiny infant before, especially one so sick. The nurse, sensing his anxiety, told him it would be fine as she handed the precious cargo into his lap and arms. She said to just relax and love her, and then she left the room.

Roberta was moved by the tenderness she saw as Harvey focused on the tiny baby in his arms. He looked as if he had just entered Heaven. After a moment he started singing, "Jesus Loves Me/ this I know."

He looked up at Robert with a big smile and said, "I think I'm in love with another woman!" They both laughed and Roberta pulled her chair closer and sat near Harvey and the baby. He spoke to her with the sweetest voice she'd ever heard coming out of his mouth.

"Roberta," he looked at her with surprise in his eyes, "let's take her home with us and we'll get her sister too." Roberta was totally shocked! Knowing the response of others who had been in this position with a sick, tiny infant, she explained to Harvey this was an emotional moment for them both, no need to even think about adoption now. The girl would have a loving foster home because she knew just who to call to foster her until a more permanent family could be found. She more than likely would have special needs, providing she even lived through these critical days. Her little body was full of the poisons of drugs and alcohol from her mother. She was low birth weight and a preemie - who knew what damage, was already done.

She also said she would check on the stepsister and find out what happened in that case and where the breakdown happened. These were the cases that gave Roberta such a reputation of never letting anything slide when it came to 'her kids'. It was another reason why she was thankful Harvey was working with the department. He was worse than she was at never letting go.

Roberta had been working to get new legislation passed and new protocols and procedures developed that would help ensure kids did not get lost in the system. Even though they were far from fixing foster care and the child protection service, each thing that was corrected and changed was another step towards closing the holes in a system that did not have the proper oversight or political support of any kind. Many of the new laws on the books were created to keep the child's best interest as the goal, not those of the parents. Roberta believed that every child born deserved an opportunity in life.

Most states mandate 'family first' regardless without regard for the evidence of what the child is experiencing. The courts had no problem disrupting a child and moving him from the only stable home he knew and placing him with a 'long-lost' relative who showed up wanting custody because they thought money was involved. Too many of these relatives were never even vetted to prove they were family. Many times, the courts would take the word of a stranger. She had seen kids moved from good homes too many times.

Many courts in today's environment have taken this to a new level since it is much easier to return the child to unworthy parenting or even a distant cousin, and simply close the case at their desk. This is what both she and Harvey were fighting against. But it was a tall order.

Some courts even were influenced by those who believed parents need not be punished for harming their children and based their opinions on the needs of those 'poor parents', giving the court a highway of leeway with their decisions. They might side with the parents even if they were drug addicts, cheating on their urine tests and lying about everything. *To hell with the kids*, the courts screamed by their actions. *They will survive. They are kids*!

There was also the constant back and forth into the system when parents just cannot parent. There were promises to these children broken over and over and drugs that were more important in the parents' lives than the slightest thought of their child.

Yes, the system was a tough one to fix and to live by where so many children have been lost and abused by the system alone, much less their parents. Roberta had committed herself from the beginning to help solve it, or at least be a part of the solution. That was why she kept climbing the ladder of management, as she quickly realized it was "authority" that worked to make things happen. It took accountability and loving the children first.

Roberta and Harvey were at a place in their lives where they could make a difference in the social services system. Yet here they were personally fighting a battle for their own lives against the very people who overwhelmed all the children with the constant crimes of drugs and greed. At least they had each other and were surefooted in their steps. The children were caught in the same web of conflict and deceit, but they rarely had anyone to turn to in their hours of need.

CHAPTER 34

HARVEY AND ROBERTA LEFT THE HOSPITAL ABOUT 2 AM on Christmas Eve morning. Roberta did what she could at the office the next day to find this baby's stepsister, but most of the department was off for the holidays and she had some trouble with the changing technology of the research systems. She only spent a couple of frustrating hours in the early morning, setting up a jump when the office opened after Christmas.

She again thought about all the children living in fear and having little or no Christmas spirit at all. The holidays brought forth bad images from years past. She shook her head and said out loud, "Don't go there Roberta," forcing herself to move on.

Roberta had been very affected by the bombing at their house. She was not on top of her game and her momentum was dwindling fast. It seemed every time she took a step forward, she was taken back three steps. Looking back, she realized she was exhausted by everything that had happened in her life since the day she met Harvey. Oh, she loved every minute of being with him, but the cartel thing had discombobulated their life, living on the edge all the time wondering if around the next corner someone was going to take a shot or another bomb would find its way to their cars or house. If she allowed herself to think about it, she would go more than crazy! She tried not to think about it at all, but even that was exhausting, constantly pushing things out of her mind. It had become a constant battle and she was battle-worn.

She finally went home to find Harvey waiting for her with dinner in the oven and a bottle of wine open and breathing. The rented house they lived in was more than beautiful at night with everyone's holiday lights shining across the water. It was almost like a postcard picture. They had decorated only sparsely for Christmas with a small fake tree and a few lights. But it was good to be home with Harvey, Velcro, and Borax.

They settled into their usual positions on the couch, side by side with both dogs between them. The dogs were panting and looking up at them with unconditional love and devotion. Roberta thought for a moment how blessed she had been to come together because of Anna.

They had a lovely evening. Harvey's roast beef was cooked like his mother used to make it. Fresh salad, vegetables, and potatoes accompanied the meal complete with garlic bread and a special dessert.

Harvey had gone by their favorite bakery while Roberta was at the office and purchased a freshly baked pecan pie with real whipped cream topping. It was Roberta's favorite of all, although she rarely allowed herself to eat sweets like this. But this was a special dinner. There was nothing he wouldn't do for her. He would have had a fresh pie flown in from the South if he thought it would make a difference to her.

Harvey's thoughts drifted back to his first marriage and how he and Cassie rarely shared times like this together. They were always at a country club or some billionaire's home for holidays. They never reached this level of intimacy in their relationship, especially during Christmas. He had loved Cassie for sure, and he never left her side when she was sick. He was thankful for her and their marriage. Yet what he had with Roberta was, well, different, special, and more than his mind ever conceived. God had been good to him in a unique way, for sure.

He thought about Gunner and his special friendship with his old partner at the law firm in Seattle. They spoke every now and then, but as with all the people they knew, they were reluctant to see friends, never wanting to put anyone in jeopardy until this cartel thing was over. At least Gunner understood, for sure. Harvey kept him in the loop.

After dinner, Roberta decided she needed to share her feelings with Harvey about her exhaustion and the discouragement she felt at how hard it was to move forward on their mission of creating a better system for kids in peril. She started talking and before long tears were rolling down both of their cheeks as she continued to share her feelings. Harvey was devastated that the most important person in his life was hurting so badly, and he had not seen it. He wanted so many times to jump in and help give solutions, but he had learned to just sit quietly and listen carefully to every word when a woman starts baring her soul. She didn't need solutions at this point. A woman in this much pain needed to vent and pour their heart out.

When she finally was done, Harvey reached over and held her for several minutes. He whispered it would be alright and how much he loved her. When he finally let her go, Roberta moved the dogs aside and nestled in her seat leaning on Harvey. Velcro seemed to understand and went immediately to the other side of Harvey. Borax couldn't understand why he was moved but Roberta placed him by her side and loved him, so he settled in.

Harvey thought to himself as they lay in each other's arms that tonight might not be the time to diagram these problems and start planning solutions. He changed the subject and got them talking about Christmases gone by. Roberta chimed in with a few stories of her own. Soon the tension relaxed, and they were both just thankful they had each other on this special and holy night.

• • •

Christmas Day broke clear and cold. They woke up together and exchanged presents, tiny gifts since they did want to add to the clutter in their rental home. Roberta helped herself to another piece of pie for breakfast as a sign of confidence. After breakfast, they drove around the area, looking at the outsides of a few of the houses that their realtor had found for them. They giggled, laughed, and dreamed together about what was next in their lives.

Harvey moved by the spirit of the holiday, commented again that they should consider filing to be a foster parent to the baby they had visited before she could be thrown into the system. Roberta reminded him that she already was in the system from birth, since all of her siblings were already there and especially since her mom abandoned her. She kissed him again for his sweetness, one of many kisses that they exchanged.

When they had settled home in the afternoon and plopped down on the ever-waiting couch, Roberta's cell phone rang. Seeing it was from the hospital, she groaned and walked into the other room to answer.

"Mrs. Waggoner, this is Renee Gray the nursing supervisor for the NICU," the crisp but cautious voice said. "I know it's Christmas and I hate to disturb you, but we have you listed as the responsible case worker for Baby Smith. I'm so sorry to inform you that Baby Smith just passed away from pneumonia. Her little underdeveloped lungs just couldn't hold on," she explained, choking slightly on the words as if she knew that they were not enough explanation. "I'm so sorry to have to ruin your Christmas celebrations with this sad news."

Roberta stood frozen for a moment before she responded. She knew how she felt about the baby, and worse still she knew how overwhelmed Harvey would feel. He seemed to love these children whom no one else wanted to love. The news would devastate him.

"Sorry for the delay, Ms. Gray," Roberta answered when she finally found her voice. "It is quite a shock after we were just holding her last night. I guess we knew how sick she was, but nothing prepares you from this kind of tragedy."

"It came up all of a sudden," the nurse explained. "The child's body was so weak, and the drugs had taken a terrible toll on her body's organs. She suffered the remainder of the night and died this morning around 11 AM. There will be a full investigation, of course," she continued, "not only from the hospital's protocols but also for the courts. You see, this could be a criminal charge against her mother. I'll file the required reports as soon as I have them and let you take care of things on your end. I thought you and Mr. Waggoner would want to know. The nurse said that your husband held her and was smiling from ear to ear."

"Yes, my husband made sure the baby knew that she was loved. Thank you for calling, Renee. And don't worry about it being Christmas. Lots of kids are spending Christmas without knowing about their parents or having someone to love them. Thank you very much for letting me know."

Harvey was sitting on the couch when she came back into the family room. "Who was that on Christmas?" he asked. He saw the look on her face and knew that the news could not be good. Roberta relayed the entire conversation and Harvey was completely shocked. He felt like someone had just sledgehammered his heart.

They both sat in silence, leaning into each other with broken hearts. "It's so odd how a little creature in need can steal your heart," Harvey said. His mind reeled back to the night he found Anna and how crippling it was when she died and now, he faced this hopeless and senseless tragedy. This was so extremely unfair! The baby never had a chance thanks to the actions of her mother.

Roberta was lost in thought thinking how she was going to find this baby's stepsister. She made mental notes of people to check with when the office opened on Monday.

CHAPTER 35

THE NEW YEAR CELEBRATION CAME AND WENT WITH-out much fanfare. Both Harvey and Roberta buried themselves in their work, Roberta looking for this baby's stepsister and Harvey diving into cases so he would not have to think about the cartel.

Harvey contacted Gunner and drove to Seattle to have lunch with him. He brought his friend up to date since the last time they spoke months ago. Gunner was amazed by the continuing mess with the cartel and suggested that they might need to relocate to another part of the country. Harvey quickly dismissed the idea since Roberta was locked in her job and all the progress she was making for kids in the state. He loved Gig Harbor but would be willing to move on his own right, although he did not really believe that would stop the cartel anyway.

Gunner meanwhile was going through a lot. He felt the pres-sure of hard work and overtime on his high-profile clients. He also had some problems at home, where his kids were growing up and becoming "more annoying," as he put it. Overall, the lunch together did them both good.

The two good friends sat at their meal for three hours and still did not want to leave, but Harvey needed to beat the horrendous traffic getting back to Gig Harbor. They agreed to meet up again the following month and even put the date in their phones. Each of them seemed to need each other in their long running friendship.

With the end of their short-term monthly lease coming up, Harvey and Roberta needed to make a housing change. They had chosen a couple of good houses but were still deciding which one they wanted. Harvey wanted to move back to Port Orchard where he could have Pete and his team available in case of a problem. But all had been quiet again and, with his law practice in Gig Harbor, he got outvoted.

Roberta had found Baby Smith's stepsister, Maci. The little girl was still in foster care, a situation which Roberta was addressing with the assigned social worker. The problem was that the foster family had several adopted kids and were not looking to adopt another. Roberta thought it was time to find the perfect permanent home for this little girl. She had been in the system since birth, much longer than expected for such a sweet girl. As all too often happened, no one had the time to focus on the child and her needs. The mother was still on the streets with outstanding warrants hanging over her head. As far as anyone could tell, she was still using drugs. But that's easy to do in the State of Washington where there are no laws against using drugs. In fact, the state furnishes fentanyl, meth, cocaine, or any other drugs to help out the homeless. This is why every homeless person in the nation hops a bus to Seattle, so they can get free drugs and sleep wherever they choose and commit crimes without fear of penalty. That's just Seattle, full of far-left liberal ideas and not big on police.

Maci's mother had been arrested not long after the newest baby died, and she even spent time in jail. Prosecutors were having a hard time making the charge hold up in court. Harvey had even tried to put some pressure on the Prosecutor, but the woman's attorneys were saying that the baby's death was no different than an abortion. In the state of Washington, the left-leaning liberals wanted the woman free even though she was responsible for her newborn child's death.

Maci deserved a chance at having a forever family and the older she got the harder it would be. This was one of those cases that captured Roberta's heart because, so far, this child had not learned to hate. She was a well-behaved little girl but had difficulty latching on to foster parents. Everyone who had kept her said she was a very sweet natured child, and even had a special "something" that placed her apart from others her age. Roberta was laser focused on finding the perfect place so that at least one child out of this dreadful family unit would have a chance at a good life with a real family.

Roberta and Harvey selected a beautiful home on the water not far from where they had been staying. Harvey called the FBI to notify them of the move, since the case was still open. He wasn't sure he should tell Roberta, so he made the call. His mission was to put this to bed and get on with life. He saw no need to upset her, so he called the FBI and asked for the agent in charge. After identifying himself, someone answered and said, "Hang up I'll call you back. Stay put." There was a disconnecting click on the phone and Harvey thought that was weird. But true to the agent's word, Harvey's phone rang within five minutes.

The FBI agent introduced himself as Special Agent Monahan. He apologized for his clandestine action on the phone, but he needed to get to a secure line. The agent asked him to proceed.

Harvey explained about the move and asked for any updates and recommendations they might have for safety preparations. He explained his frustrations since this had been going on way too long and he felt like he had been left out of the information loop.

To Harvey's surprise since he thought Pete was keeping him updated, Monahan admitted that there had been a lot going on with this case. In fact, they were closing in on what they thought might be a leak from the FBI. The agent asked to come and search the house before they moved in so the field agents would know its layout. Although Harvey had never heard his name before, Special Agent Monahan turned out to be the agent in charge of the case. He went on to explain that this was a huge operation, much larger than earlier expected. The ties of this specific ring have led to Congress and even the Canadian Parliament. Harvey was stunned as he realized why it had taken so long. There had been leaks not only in the FBI, but also in the Sheriff's department. Very few people knew anything about the case because of the leaders involved.

The FBI figured that the cartel has kept tabs on Harvey in part because he had embarrassed one of the bosses, but mainly because they were convinced that he had knowledge about the drugs in the car. Special Agent Monahan felt that there was someone inside the Port Orchard Sheriff's department that was at Ground Zero when the drug bust took place.

"At first," explained the agent, "whoever the inside person is tried to pin the drug deal on you. When it was clear that didn't work, they tried to scare you to give them time to recover the product so they decided they would scare you off, but that didn't work either. After a couple of attempts, the decision went up the chain of command and a complete hit was ordered. The cartel's failure to complete their job has only added more push. Trust me Harvey, the extermination order is still in play. They have a contract out to kill you."

The FBI was still unsure how the pieces all fit together, and it had taken a long time because of the nature of trust within the Sheriff's department. Monahan added this warning, "We advise you NOT to discuss or disclose any of this conversation, or even tell my name to your friend Pete Murdock. If the cartel's source in the Sheriff's office finds out, you may be in even more danger. The FBI can't afford to lose our element of surprise, or we might also lose any leads and connections to who's pulling the strings and financing this venture. Those are the guys we really want."

When Harvey heard that his heart and soul sunk. He felt that he had just lost a good and trusted friend. If Pete was the cartel's connection, Harvey would make sure he went down. Pete had put his family in danger while continuing to act as a friend. Now Harvey began to think back on every conversation the two men had had.

Special Agent Monahan went over in detail all the things that had occurred with Harvey and how each time it gave the FBI more information. "I'm glad you finally reached out to us. We couldn't risk contacting you without letting Officer Murdock or the Sheriff's office know we were still in the field. We're not sure if the Sheriff's office, or even Pete Murdock is involved, but we've noticed that Pete always seems to be near the scene of any attempt against you. And the criminals are always one step ahead of law enforcement. The Sheriff's office is the logical place for the leaks to be coming from."

Harvey shook his head in disbelief. It felt like he was facing years of lies. Monahan went on to confirm that there were some big names, both in the state and across both the USA and Canada, who would be at risk if this ring ever was expose. "There are a lot of wealthy and powerful people in on this, politicians, and even judges. These guys will spare nothing or no one to keep the money coming in. The name of the game is moving drugs, especially fentanyl, and sex trafficking along the west coast. These are highly profitable businesses. We've slowed this cartel run down a little with our initial raids, but that was just a small piece of the puzzle. If we can get some of the big names down, we can stop a large part of the trade."

Harvey was hardly breathing, unable to believe what he was hearing. He was more worried about Roberta since her activities did so much to block the traffickers from abusing the child protective system. Harvey explained his worries, asking Special Agent Monahan if he should tell his wife.

"Most definitely, if she is trustworthy," the agent said. "We of course know a lot about your wife too. You both need to be on your toes as this case is coming to a head, which is why I took your call today. I would have reached out to you very soon anyway. We already knew you were moving just waiting till you selected a house and then we would have made contact."

"There is one more thing," warned Monahan. "Do not change your behaviors or patterns right now. They're watching you and we're watching them."

They finished their conversation with instructions for Harvey not to call the Bureau directly again, Monahan would make contact. He would have an electrician come out to their house, something would surely need to be done before the move, and they would wire the house. Also, Monahan would provide Harvey with a "burner" phone in case they needed to talk.

Harvey was shaken by the time they hung up, his mind roiling with scenarios. He hated all of this, reflecting on the night it had all begun. He thought how trapped Anna's mother must have felt, knowing her danger but not aware of everything that was going on. At least he knew the risks and felt that they had a chance at getting out of this alive. He had no intention of letting the traffickers win.

CHAPTER 36

THAT EVENING ROBERTA AND HARVEY HAD PLANNED to visit the house one more time and meet with the Realtor to sign the sales contract to purchase their incredible new home. Roberta was so excited about having her own place again, she was giddy. Harvey did his best to put a happy face forward, but Roberta knew him too well. She knew he was disturbed about something. By now, she understood that if he was holding back, it was for her good. He would tell her everything in time. She made a mental note to ask him about it later.

The house they purchased was a showstopper. It sat on the water looking at the Cascade Mountain range and all the boat traffic passing by. The magnificent property was on an inlet lined with beautiful homes. The previous owners had taken great care and mostly everything had been updated. Roberta was beyond excited to get moved and start to decorate.

She would need to do a few things with the property for the dogs, but fortunately, during their time at the rental house Velcro and Borax had learned to stay in the backyard without a fence. She needed to reinforce their sense of boundary again in the new home. The openness of the backyard to the water seemed to be the only thing Harvey didn't like about the house into their house. It just gave more opportunities for criminals to find a way in. But they were buying for the rest of their lives, for a time hopefully when there would be no more cartels trying to get at them. The minute they had walked into this house he saw that Roberta was "in love" and that any concerns or criticisms he had were null and void.

The offer was submitted and accepted within hours. They had gotten a call at home that the contract was done and accepted with no changes, and closing would be set up right away. They discussed options. Harvey pushed out the closing a little, not knowing when the FBI 'electrician' would be available.

That night after dinner, with the contracts signed and their new home waiting for them, they sat in their familiar places on the couch and Roberta announced that she had good news. She was smiling like he'd never seen before.

"We can use some good news," Harvey answered, relieved to not have to talk about his conversation with the FBI. "And you're acting like you just passed some protocol or saved a hundred children. What's going on?"

"Not that many," she said inscrutably. "Only today I got a notice that Maci Smith is back in the system again. Remember her?"

"That beautiful baby's stepsister. Of course, I remember her. So horribly sad!" said Harvey.

"Well, maybe or maybe not," she said with a grin.

BROKEN TRUST: CHILDREN IN PERIL

"What are you up to, Mrs. Waggoner?" Harvey asked with a n intrigued chuckle.

"Well, Maci will be up for adoption, now" she said stopping and looking deep into his eyes for some signs of understanding."

"Okay, is that a good thing or bad thing?" Harvey asked.

"Harvey Waggoner, for such a smart man, you can be so thick sometimes. It can be a very good thing if you're open to the idea."

Harvey's brain had already been fried enough today. He was so nervous that he wanted nothing to do with guessing games. "What idea?" he asked.

"Harvey, what would you say if we were to adopt Maci? She's about three now and she's never had a permanent home since she was born. She's a troublesome child even. And well, you and I seem to fall in love with these children in need. You held her half-sister, one of the few people who ever gave her love in her short life. That would an important connection to her. I really think we could help this little girl by providing her a forever home. What do you say?" She paused to gauge his reaction but only received a blank stare.

"We could do this, Harvey," Roberta pleaded "We couldn't save Anna or Maci's sister, but we can save Maci."

Harvey knew he would have to tell her about his conversation with the FBI even though it might destroy Roberta's joy. He desperately wanted to adopt this child, but he was hesitant to bring a child into this mess.

Roberta sensed his reluctance and wondered if she had misread his passions all along. "Harvey? What's wrong with you? I thought Maci's adoption was a gift that both you and I have wanted for a long time. You were the one who wanted to claim both the girls. We've talked about giving a child in need a forever home and you look terrified by the idea."

"Look," he said, tears brimming in his eyes. "We need to talk about something I wanted to put off, at least until we were safe in our new house. Of course, I would love to have a little girl, especially one that needs us. I want Maci to be ours in the worst way. But the timing couldn't be worse."

He poured them each another glass of wine. The dogs instinctually knew there was going to be a long discussion and settled in with their masters as Harvey began unwrapping the story.

Harvey talked through the entire situation about the cartel's activity and their own exposure. Roberta took it as she did every challenge, with a brave face and the courage to fight. She loved breaking challenges apart piece by piece and finding solutions.

Several hours later they realized they had not eaten dinner. Roberta jumped up and said, "Let me fix us a sandwich. I have some potato salad left over, too." She put it all together and brought it on a tray over to the couch. Harvey had opened another bottle of wine and was waiting for her with glass and bottle in hand.

Harvey explained they would both need to get out on the practicing range again to perfect their shooting if they needed to go that far. Both had concealed weapons permits and they each intended to carry a weapon in case they were separated or kidnapped. Who knows what this level of crime these people would do?

Together they devised a plan. They would each perfect their shooting skills and, since they both had concealed weapon permits, they would stay armed at all times. They also agreed they should hire their own security to watch the new house for a while, if Special Agent Monahan was in agreement. Harvey knew that the FBI was supposed to be watching them, but he felt that their emphasis was more on capturing the criminals than on protecting either of them.

"What about Maci?" Roberta asked in a sad, tired voice. "I don't want her to go to yet another foster home where they have no intention of adopting her. I want her, Harvey. We need her!" Tears streamed down her face.

"I know we both need her," he answered. "And she needs us. So why don't you go ahead to get the paperwork started? I'm tired of living my life by the cartel's rules. Keep in mind, Roberta, absolutely no one should know about these new developments for any reason. 'We'll have to work around inspections and all until we get this cartel thing behind us. Just be careful because telling the wrong person could cost us our lives and now the life of a child." He was still deeply concerned about bringing Maci home, but he also didn't want to lose her either.

It had been raining off and on for several weeks. After all it is the Pacific Northwest where they are known for gray days and rain. But on this day, they awoke to sunshine and beautiful skies.

Roberta walked to the window looking at a beautiful view, and pronounced, "Harvey, today is the day. This is the day where everything goes right for us, and we will find the answers we need to go forward." Her smile beamed from ear to ear.

"Have you been talking with God or something?" he asked, grinning along with her. "I haven't seen this side of you in forever, my dear wife."

"Maybe I have," she said. "Maybe your connection with God and prayer is finally having an impact on my life. I decided I'd give it a try." She smiled at his look of shocked surprise. "I do remember how to pray, you know. I WAS raised in a fanatical religious home, after all. I didn't forget everything I learned as a child. I just wanted to forget the parents who drove me to reject all the good things I learned." She said smiling as she walked to the bathroom to shower. "You've got nothing on me there, cowboy!" laughing as she closed the bathroom door.

CHAPTER 37

D ESPITE THE COMBINED TRAUMA OF THE ADOPTION
and the cartel's rising threat in their lives, things moved along
nicely. They had a long talk about options if anything went sideways, developing strategic plans for everything from a home inva-
sion to discovering another bomb. Now, they added plans for how
they would protect Maci.

And it wasn't just the risk to the family that filled their plans.
They started to discuss how their lives would change on a daily basis
with a child filling their days. In spite of the overcast cloud of the
cartel, they began gaining excitement. Roberta was right; it was a
good, good day.

Over the next month, they moved into their new home, working and juggling schedules to meet contractors, decorators, and all
the rest. When all the contractor work was done, Harvey and Roberta
finally had a home that was beyond their wildest imagination with
the perfect, breathless view of the beautiful Cascades. The adoption
process progressed smoothly, filling their days with new excitement
and anticipation. Even though they were living through hell inside

their minds, both Roberta and Harvey were functioning at the top of their game.

The couple had developed great reputations regarding their work. It was amazing how fast and far news traveled. Roberta was offered a national job with the CPS Social Services system and politely declined. She wanted to stay where she could make the most difference. Her job was going well, and she and Harvey were finally breaking the stream of parents pulling the wool over the eyes of CPS and the courts. Harvey too had multiple offers from power areas like New York, Michigan, and even Texas but he likewise turned them all down. Harvey had even been asked to run for state office, but he quickly declined that as well.

In the long run, both of them felt they could do more good in a very liberal state like Washington where they felt no one was watching out for unwanted children. Being a catalyst for these kids was what each of them had dreamed about all their lives. The connections they had all over the country brought new ideas and resources along the way. Finally, each in their own way was effecting change for the lives of abused and abandoned kids.

• • •

After another conversation with the Special Agent Monahan, Harvey became more suspicious of his good friend Officer Pete. Between the facts that Monahan had shared and the things that he heard from the policeman, things just didn't add up. Although neither said anything, both men felt the strain on their friendship. It was an awkward feeling for Harvey, particularly since that friend had saved his life already once.

Harvey hated to think about it. It just wasn't right to be suspicious of a friend. But he lived in fear lest anyone, even Pete, discover what he really knew about the case. He even began to suspect the FBI, wondering if their breech had reached Monahan. He still could not understand why the cartel thought he was involved in any way with the murder of Anna's mother and or the stolen drugs. None of it made sense. Either Monahan had failed to share something that would make the pieces of this puzzle fit together or he was a dirty agent.

Since the very first night, he had gone over events a thousand times wondering what he did to put suspicion on himself. What did they see? What did they think they saw? When did he have an opportunity to do anything at all against them?

In desperation, he had even reached out to an old fraternity brother who was a federal judge and asked a few probing questions. His sharp fraternity brother said, "Harvey, the questions you're asking me are really weird, even for you. Are you in a position where you can't say anything? Is this why all the random questions?" Harvey responded with silence, so the judge stopped asking questions and told him about times he had encountered similar criminal situations. His stories alone probably helped Harvey more than anything in understanding that there are so many layers within a large criminal syndicate that anything was possible. His friend explained he had overseen cases where an innocent bystander was the victim of retaliation by the cartel for no reason at all.

After that conversation, Harvey began to relax his paranoia a little, but he still harbored suspicions which he hated. Before the conversation with Special Agent Monahan, he and Pete had been meeting every couple of weeks for coffee. Since that time, Harvey had not returned any of Pete's calls and they had not met professionally or socially. Pete worried that Harvey had reached his breaking point and did not even want to talk about the situation, so he was very guarded about the information he now offered. Harvey found Pete's sudden silence even more worrisome. So, the circle of suspicion went around.

Harvey needed to keep his mind clear of this kind of thinking. He had a daughter arriving in the next month or so. Roberta worked on Maci's room as he checked out private preschools and sports activities for her to be involved with. She was still so young, but Harvey was excited about the future. He could coach soccer, basketball, baseball, tennis, you name it. He wanted to share in the life of his little girl. At the same time, he knew her safety would be up to him, but he felt up for the job.

Roberta and Harvey had met with Maci several times and with the case supervisor's permission even taken her out for ice cream once. They adored her and she seemed to respond well to their attention. She had obvious abandonment issues since no family had kept her for long. None of the family issues had been due to behavior. There was a clear record that she had been perfect wherever she had been. In fact, Harvey thought this little girl was so much smarter than people gave her credit for. She had something going on in that little brain. *She's a real 'problem solver'*, Harvey thought. *She may have special needs, alright, but her specialness might swing towards the brilliant side.* Harvey was intrigued by her.

Roberta had told Harvey the main reason for her placement uncertainty was the fact that the families she resided with were seasoned foster homes but had no interest in adoption. Occasionally one or two of these families might adopt a certain child, but then they would need to opt out of foster care as their house would be full of their own children. Whatever social worker was on the case knew Maci's record and the number of times she had been moved, but she had four different social workers in her three young years and there was never consistency here either. They had never been able to take the time to find a foster home that might be able to adopt either because there were too many children or because of financial issues. In short, Maci's timing had sucked. She just hit these great homes at the wrong time.

At last, the day came when they were picking up Maci for good. They had been in their new home for a couple of months with all the security in place. The official court approved adoption would not occur for a while yet, but everything was completed from their end. They had managed to get through the process without revealing anything about the cartel situation. Roberta had struggled with not being perfectly honest, but their lives were at stake, and they knew every possible protection had been put in place to ensure the safety of this child at home.

Both Harvey and Roberta had taken three weeks' vacation to acclimate Maci to her new home and new dogs. Maci was finally getting a new family that she would never have to leave. Harvey had already made up his mind that she would not be allowed to date until she was 35! He had fallen so deeply in love with the child that he had no idea he wasn't the biological dad.

As they pulled up in front of the house where Maci had been staying, they looked at each other and said in unison, "This is it! We're going to be parents!"

Little Maci was waiting at the door for them. She pushed open the screen door and began running to them. Roberta bent down and swooped her up in her arms, kissing her all over. Maci held out her arms for Harvey and his heart melted again. They thanked the foster family for taking such good care of her and preparing her for this moment. While they knew she could not completely understand, they all could tell the little angel knew in her heart things would be okay.

The first thing Maci asked for was ice cream. The new family got in the car and drove off to the nearest creamery and to the life that waited for them together.

CHAPTER 38

FOR TOO LONG NOW, ROBERTA AND HARVEY KNEW that each night without a new threat was a blessing. Now things were different. They had a child. Harvey lay awake the night they picked Maci up, thinking about how awesome he felt to be a dad. He could not have been happier. In fact, the night was sleepless for both knew parents as they listened for any sounds from Maci's room. Both dogs piled on the bed to protect the little girl, as if they instantly knew that she belonged to their family and that their job was to make sure they were there for her.

For a foster child who had been moved numerous times from one home to another, Maci was amazing. Most important, she felt safe, especially with the dogs at the end of her bed. Maci seemed to feel like she belonged immediately. She giggled for more than a half hour when she met Velcro and Borax. They licked her clean of any germs, for sure, and she loved every minute of it. They followed her around all night, Velcro on one side and Borax flanking the other. Harvey was amazed that two dogs who had never been around children took to her so quickly. Maci somehow knew how to be gentle with them as if she'd been raised around dogs her whole life. Harvey took this as one more sign that the prayers he had made every night for Maci's safety and happiness were being answered.

Maci awoke at around 6 AM and was greeted by her new Dad carrying her to the breakfast table. Roberta was fixing animal pancakes with whipped cream and strawberries. Maci was so excited.

As she finished her pancakes and Harvey and Roberta were contentedly breakfasting on coffee and English muffin, the doorbell rang.

Harvey got up and went to the door to find Special Agent Monahan there. The muffin turned to lead in his stomach.

"Harvey, I need to speak with you," said the agent. "Can we chat on the porch?"

Harvey stepped through the door quietly and closed it behind him. Roberta noticed and instantly got alarmed. She hurried up Maci to finish and ushered her into the bathroom to start her morning routine of bathing, brushing her teeth, combing her hair, and getting dressed. By the time she was slipping on Maci's tennis shoes, Harry stepped into the bedroom and nodded for Roberta to join him.

Roberta called the dogs to come into the room and opened the new toy chest for Maci to discover. She asked the girl to make her bed and told her she would be back in a minute after she talked to Daddy.

Roberta joined Harry in the hallway, closing the door part way so Maci would not be scared. Harvey told her she needed to grab a bag with whatever she and Mac needed for the day and get in the car with the dogs. They quickly dressed for the day and went to Maci's room, smiling as they told her they were going on an adventure. Within less than 30 minutes, they were in the car taking off somewhere; they'd figure it out as they went. The dogs were excited to find Maci's seat in the back with them as they took up their positions on each side of her.

As they drove, Harvey explained to Roberta that the Monahan had told him that the FBI had it on good authority that there was going to be a hit today from the cartel. The agent had promised to keep in touch with the burner phone and advised him not to tell anyone what was going on, especially his friend Pete Murdock.

Harvey suspicions flared up again. He couldn't imagine that Pete was involved as he had always been there to help Harvey and Roberta. They trusted him. Harvey thought to himself, *I can't go down that rabbit hole. There is no proof of anything. God help us if Pete is in on this.* His dark thoughts were quickly interrupted with giggling and barking. Maci was playing with the dogs, and they were having a ball.

They quickly discussed some options before they got on the freeway and decided they would start at the dog park to let the dogs wear themselves out. Maci could play on the monkey bars and swings while Harvey and Roberta could work out what to do next.

Just as they reached, his phone rang. It was Monahan shouting, "Harvey, get out of the car immediately! There's a bomb attached to it! The police are on their way with the bomb squad!" said the agent. Harvey pulled into the parking lot and hustled everyone over to a safe place behind some large trees. He shouted to everyone nearby to head for cover.

Within seconds of reaching the woods, a huge explosion occurred and debris flew everywhere. The car was blown to pieces but all the family and both dogs were safe. Maci was screaming and crying as she held onto Roberta for dear life. Velcro ran towards Harvey while Borax stayed at Maci's side. When Velcro reached Harvey, she jumped into his waiting arms. His first thought was what a beautiful picture she was of the true love of a dog and protector. The shock and horror hit him and he began sobbing. *What have I done?* He thought. *How have I brought my family into this mess?*

He could hear the sirens coming close, but they were too late. Now all he wanted was revenge. His anger had tipped to the point of blind rage. His life had been turned upside down by these criminals and he didn't even know why. No one was giving him answers, just problems. He was getting to the bottom of this even if he had to go meet the mastermind of this cartel group. He was done trusting people.

The police quickly contained the area while the fire department put out the burning car. The explosion broke windows in the cars parked around them and debris fell all around the lot. Everywhere, people were crying out loud rushing towards their cars. Terrified children screamed throughout the park. Fortunately, because of Harvey's quick efforts, no one in the park had been injured. For that he was eternally thankful!

Harvey ordered Velcro to go back and protect the family. Roberta had Maci calmed down a little, and they were sitting on the ground with the child in her arms and the dogs watching all sides. People were beginning to go back to their cars as the police were out combing the parking lot.

Harvey's eyes were sweeping everywhere to make sure everyone was safe and if he could see any familiar cars. He had just about convinced himself there was nothing there when, out of the corner of his eye. he saw the dark sedan and what he thought was Sheriff Bloom.

He thought, *wait a minute, this is Pierce County not Kitsap County where he was Sheriff. How was Bloom on the FBI notification list*?

He squinted his eyes again as if to clear them out and saw the car slowly pulling away out the only open exit of the park. All entrances and exits had been blocked by police cars but the car was slowly slithering out. Harvey knew instantly that something was wrong. He looked back at his family giving them and Velcro the 'stay' sign and started running toward the car. He saw the car speeding up a bit so Harvey ran with everything he had and screamed, "Stop that car!"

At the moment the sedan reached the only exit, two unidentified cars slammed beside it, stopping it in its tracks. Two men jumped out of the car with guns pointed and screamed, "FBI! Hands in the air!"

Harvey stopped his frantic run when he saw Agent Monahan and three police officers, all with guns drawn, pull the driver from the car, take away his weapon, and shove his head down on the front of the car as they applied handcuffs.

As the man turned around, Harvey could see that it *was* Sheriff Bloom. He began running toward the man in anger and confusion. "Did you do this to my family?" he screamed at the man. The Sheriff locked eyes with him and gave him a smirk.

Special Agent Monahan, putting his weapon in his holster, walked toward Harvey. He saw how angry he was and didn't want him any closer. With Monahan gently restraining him, Harvey saw the FBI unit push Bloom into a car and speed off down the road.

Harvey was in complete rage as he ran screaming at him, shouting, "What's next, Mr. G-man? Are they going to blow up this house too? Exactly when were you going to tell me about the bomb?

What the hell do you guys do, showing up after something is blown up? When are you going to stop watching and do something to make us safe?" He stomped his foot in rage.

"I'm sick of being Mr. Nice Guy and trusting you idiots!" he continued his rant. "It's time I had some answers NOW! To start with, what the hell was the Sheriff doing here and why did you just arrest him? Did the Sheriff's office conjure up this whole thing?

Special Agent Monahan allowed him to finish running off and then quietly said, "Harvey, please get in my car for a minute. I want to tell you something." Harvey reluctantly got in the car, glancing over at Roberta and noticed Maci was lying in her lap and the dogs were still on guard. He gave her a wave to reassure her and then followed the FBI agent into his car.

Monahan began to calmly lay out the story. First, he assured Harvey that his home had been looked over by the bomb experts and there was no bomb there. They had found a bomb with a timing device on Roberta's car which had already been disarmed and removed. "They were very clever," he said. "They would have had you, no matter which care you tried to escape in. I guess the Sheriff wanted to ensure the job was done right this time."

Monahan went on to confirm that Anna's mother had taken her baby and was running from her abusive boyfriend who was one of the leaders of the cartel group. He also explained that the car was loaded with drugs, weapons, and a sizeable amount of cash.

"Cash?" Harvey asked. "This is the first I've ever heard about cash. What does that mean?"

"Here's the good part, the part I couldn't disclose until now." Monahan took a deep breath, looking around outside the car to make sure no one was listening, and then he continued. "Harvey, when you discovered the car, it happened to be just when the cartel had arrived to retrieve the items in the car. They saw you pull up, waited, and watched you from the woods as best as they could. They certainly didn't want to be seen by you. They drove away when they heard the sirens. They were watching long enough to see that you open the car door to check on the mother and the baby. They would have killed her if she wasn't already dead and would also have finished off the child, but you and the police kept them from completing the job. In essence you saved that child's life that night," he said kindly.

Yeah, I did I guess only for her to die with the evidence of their drugs in her body, Harvey thought tearing up again.

The FBI agent continued, "You're aware the Mexican cartels reach goes up the political ladder to the White House and in many law enforcement headquarters. Right? How do you think they are so successful and rarely caught? How do you think with all the sex trafficking and drugs have been so successful?"

"They saw you climbing in the back and pulling out a bag. They couldn't be sure you had found anything, but they assumed you did. Obviously, you were too traumatized by the baby's screaming and the whole scene to even notice anything else in the car. But they didn't know that. In their minds they thought you knew, and even that you had taken some of their goods out of the car. They investigated you through your car and found out that you were a high-powered lawyer whose firm happened to represent some of their clients, it doesn't matter who right now. They figured you had been tipped off about the money, drugs, and guns. The woman in the car had no idea that she was carrying anything. She was target as a potential leak and they just ran her off the road and beat her to death. The baby in back must have been a huge surprise to them. We think they were under the impression that she left the girl somewhere when she fled. Ironically, the woman had stopped to ask for help at the very police department that betrayed her."

Harvey lifted his head and said, "The Port Orchard Police and Sheriff's office? Does that mean that Pete is in on all this?"

Monahan shook his head. "Not Pete personally, but someone on duty was helping the Sheriff cover up the heist and then tried to blame it on you, as best we can find out. The Sheriff has been on the Cartel's payroll since California. When the woman showed up at the station, whoever it was recognized her and called in Sheriff Bloom, we assume to let him know the product was on the run. So, at the very least, that officer was in bed with the Sheriff on this. Sadly, we now have clear evidence that Bloom was the leader of the cover-up. He didn't want the Cartel finding out he took the money. He wasn't stupid enough to take the drugs and guns because he can't fence them. His only option was fingering you for the cartel to keep the heat off himself, and of course keep the money."

All of a sudden, the pieces of the puzzle came flying together, dropping into place to make a clear picture. Harvey understood why his house had been torn apart in the first place, looking to see if Harvey did in fact have anything from the car. Why they were always one step ahead of Pete and everyone else. Pete was reporting all his progress to his boss, who would send the information to members of the cartel gang. The Sheriff needed a fall guy. He was the perfect candidate.

"Just so you know," Monahan continued. "We got wind there would be a bomb somewhere. That was no dress rehearsal. A person of interest was seen leaving your house and our agents assumed they planted a bomb. We had no idea of the timeline, just wanted you and your family out of that house so we could give it a go over. We just had no idea that they had tampered with the cars until we found a piece of what looked like a bomb pin in your garage and found the bomb on your wife's car. That was when we realized that they had been "booby trapped" your cars and I called you. Just in time, I guess."

"As to Sheriff Bloom showing up at the scene, well that was a surprising gift," said Monahan, looking closely at Harvey. "We are assuming he knew we were zooming in on his office and he had to ensure this bombing would lock it up. He kept Pete out the loop entirely. My guess is Pete knows now and is on his way to see it for himself. He's a loyal friend, you know."

His eyes scanned the wreckage in the parking lot and he shrugged. "Anyway, within moments after getting the bomb threat we finally connected proof of the Sheriff's involvement. He'd had already taken the $250,000 cash for his efforts, leaving the guns and drugs behind for us to work with. We only knew about the cash through an informant we found recently. Once the evidence against the Sheriff was found and locked in, we had a tracker put on his vehicles at home and his squad car. That's how we followed him to this park. Our officers arrived at the Sheriff's office about an hour ago, and we're trying to cut a deal with the other involved officer to put Bloom away for a long while."

Harvey breathed for the first time since the bombing and said, "I'm just glad to hear that Pete wasn't involved. That would have killed me," he said. He shook his head at the irony of the statement, having been so close to death so often during the last two years.

Monahan nodded. "We knew about your friendship with Pete and knew we had to get him out of the loop, so we fed him some bad information and then took ownership of the case," he said. "It worked out this time, but it's not always this good of an ending. I doubt the carte 1 will bother you anymore. The suspicion has been placed on the Sheriff now and we're pretty sure the cartel is aware that you possess nothing of theirs. Just don't expect any apologies or flowers from them," chortling as he said it. He smiled and stuck out his hand for a trusting handshake. "Although, this case will remain open maybe for years, you're stuck with me if anything happens down the road."

Harvey got further instructions on what to say to the media if he was interviewed, as well as the assurance that the FBI would be keeping an eye out daily for a while until they were sure the coast was clear. He opened the car door and got out as if he was seeing the world for the first time. Roberta could see from his body language even from a distance that things had been resolved.

CHAPTER 39

H ARVEY WALKED BACK TOWARDS HIS FAMILY AS VELCRO ran to him like he'd been shot out of a cannon. He bent down to grab the good dog and hugged and kissed her, making up for lost time.

Maci was still asleep, so Harvey sat down with Roberta and started telling her the whole story. Before he was finished, he looked up and saw a familiar face walking towards them. When Velcro saw it was Pete, she went running for him with her tail wagging.

Harvey called out, "Pete, my friend. How did you get here so fast again?" said he stood up and embraced his friend. Pete smiled then knelt down to greet Roberta where she sat with her little beauty asleep on her lap.

Harvey joined them on the ground. "I'm so sorry I was late again after the action, but I've been fed a bunch of crap contributing to us losing communication these last few months. I was in a really bad place and didn't know who to believe or where to turn. I should never have doubted you, Pete. Please forgive me." Harvey stuck out his hand in friendship and trust.

"Don't give it another thought, man," said Pete sincerely, taking the hand and squeezing it. "I knew things didn't add up for me. I guessed the FBI had you in lock down, but I was still concerned because I didn't like the direction this entire thing was leaning."

The three started catching up. The first business was to tell Pete all about Maci. He had never met her and had only just heard about her adoption when Harvey had been forced into radio silence. He couldn't keep his eyes off how beautiful she was and said she looked a little bit like Roberta.

Then they sighed and talked about the end of their dangerous game. Pete shook his head and said, "I've got to say, I never, ever expected my boss, who I thought was my friend, would be involved with the cartel. I guess money and greed can take the most well-intentioned man to the brink of destruction. These were the very people we had been fighting against for years on the I-5 drug highway. I feel betrayed and lied to, and he put my friends in harm's way. But you guys were amazing through it all, to say nothing about Velcro and how she was always so strong and courageous. I've said it before, Harvey. Anytime you want to work for the police force, we will hire you. I know for a fact that there is a Sheriff position open," Pete joked.

As they shared some tired laughter, Roberta's phone rang, which startled her. She was still on leave but it was her assistant calling. Roberta's smile widened with great interest as she promised to stop by later in the afternoon.

Harvey was curious but knew her work was very private and didn't want to ask any questions. All he said was, "I hope that was something positive you just heard about. We've had enough traumas from one day. Heck, for a lifetime!"

Roberta gave him a look he didn't quite understand, then Maci woke up and spent some time talking with Pete until they decided they all wanted to go home. Oddly enough, Maci never questioned what happened. Roberta guessed that this poor child had been through so many traumas in her life, so many transfers from home to home, so many broken promises, so many new people taking over her life, she was just glad that she woke up with her dogs and her mommy and daddy. No personal changes here. She just giggled and hugged the dogs.

Later on, Roberta would take the time to explain in simple terms about bad guys and how sometimes they try and hurt people. But Daddy and Pete had made sure the bad guy was caught and locked away, so she didn't have to worry anymore. She was safe.

Pete stood up with them. "Let me give you a ride back to your house. I don't think your car is going to start," he said laughing.

Harvey groaned but smiled back. "Way too soon, man," he said. "But I completely forgot about that, Pete. Thanks for continuing to keep my brain in gear. You've always been dependable that way." He gave his friend a pat on the back as they walked over to Pete's car.

They all piled into Pete's SUV and headed home. "Just so you know," he said. "I've verified once again with the FBI agents that your house is clean and Roberta's car is fine and completely disarmed."

Roberta nodded solemnly. "Thank you, Pete. I've got to say, it's scary just getting into a car right now." She and Harvey held hands across the back seat and front seats. Velcro put his head on the cradle of the couple's arms and everyone broke out laughing.

CHAPTER 40

AS THEY WERE PULLING UP TO THEIR HOME, PETE stopped the car and looked at Harvey and Roberta. You could see the misty eyes and look of compassion of what this couple had been through. The betrayal by his Chief was another matter totally, he would deal with that emotion later.

"Harvey, Roberta, I know I've said this already, but I do want you to know how sorry I am for all of this destruction in your lives. Removing that from the equation, I am thankful I've met both of you and while I am sorry about Anna's death, it brought the two of you together and now look at you." He said with pride.

"I've especially loved getting to know and love Velcro! You have yourself a fine watchdog in that little shepherd. I'd like to hear the story one day of how she got her name!" They all laughed as Pete drove into the driveway of their lovely home.

They parted ways promising to get together for a BBQ before the good weather ended. Pete wanted his wife and kids to meet these very important people in his life. They had come through a lot and

Pete was not going to let go of his new friends and their growing family.

Back at the house, two dogs and a child went inside and was ecstatic, Maci was ecstatic. In her entire young life, she had never known if she was coming back to the same place. Now she was at her forever home. Roberta and Maci took her outside to throw rocks in the water, with the dogs' help of course. Roberta stared at her in silence thanking God for this angel in her life. She knew all too well how many times Maci had been moved, sometimes even sleeping through being moved, so she woke up in a strange house. Roberta knew that she had homes with foster parents who were only in care for the money – the younger the child, the more money they got. One set of foster parents had even locked her in a closet and left for the entire day. It was a dark closet where no one heard her cries.

At other times she had been slapped across the room, whipped with a wire, and even burned with cigarettes. The child never knew if she would see another day. But Maci was exceptional; she learned to live in a fantasy world when things got rough. Rather than turning bitter and hateful, she made the choice at her young age to be happy even if she had to pretend that things were okay.

What discipline and brain power God had blessed Maci to embrace! Roberta understood and was amazed by the child's complexity. She had been working with abused and abandoned kids for a long time. It had not been merely a job; it was a purpose for her life. She had tried and tried to change the rules, to bring attention to these unwanted children. She felt she had accomplished only a small step. She still needed to get political power behind her to bring the broken system new life and really help these children.

This child, now her child, had a tremendously bad start in life all because her mother chose drugs and selling her body for the next fix over her own daughter. The woman had done the same to all her children. Somehow, by God's grace, Maci had made it through. Somehow, she had never learned to act out. Somehow, she still had the capacity to love. Somehow, she still had trust. Maybe one day all the memories would come rushing back and change her completely. There are many stories of that occurring in small children who were moved from house to house. But Roberta would always be on alert for those signs.

Roberta thought about all the children that the system failed. She could not save many because of antiquated laws or rules, or the lack thereof. Some of these children who had experiences like Maci turn into very distrusting, hate-filled kids who were out to harm others like they were harmed. The school shootings and violent crimes committed by children and teens are proof of that. When you lose trust, love, and a sense of loving yourself, this frequently occurs. Many kids' fates are due to abuses not being discovered, sometimes because social workers are overworked, understaffed, and underpaid. The haphazard nature of the care system caused missteps all the time. It is as if there is no one that cares about children anymore.

Roberta did care, without question, and she would keep fighting for everyone that came under her umbrella, not just the children but also the workers who had to live and apply their skills in the system. She was well known as a mentor, but she was also a good friend. There are many people leading the Social Service systems with her attitude and care, but sometimes attitude just is not enough. The at-risk kids need more resources. Roberta reminded herself she was in one of the states in the country that was hardest on children.

Because of the state's mostly liberal views, the courts rule most often in favor of the parents getting one chance after the other. They are given free rehab that never works, free food, free drugs; almost everything is handed to these parents in the hopes that they will succeed and be good parents. It is no secret that parents know they are more likely to keep their kids and their drugs in the state of Washington. But Roberta worked day and night to improve the odds a little bit with whatever control she had under her power.

Maci and Roberta came in from outside and began fixing some lunch while Harvey and Special Agent Monahan were still chatting and looking at paperwork. It had been a big day for Maci, so Roberta put her in bed for a nap and she instantly went to sleep. She was so thankful that Maci was a gifted little girl, fearless and powerful in her own way, but she also knew she would still need counseling to keep away the thoughts and memories she had locked away in her little mind. *A thought for another time,* Roberta said to herself as she kissed her daughter on the forehead.

Without warning, Roberta grabbed her bag and kissed Harvey as she headed to the door. "I'll be back in an hour. I just need to sign some papers at work."

Ah, Harvey thought to himself, *she's off to save another child. When will this woman slow down?"*

Harvey went in to check on Maci who was fast asleep. The dogs raised their heads to see if they had new orders, but Harvey told them to stay with Maci. "Keep watch," he whispered to them as he went into the kitchen to grab a bite.

As he was eating his sandwich and reviewing the events of the day then suddenly started crying. The sound of the sobs brought

Velcro to his master to see what was going on. He had just felt so overwhelmed by it all and so helpless to protect his family. The sudden emotions were a big surprise, but he reassured himself he needed the release and to get it over with. *Look at Roberta*, he thought. *She has not bent even the slightest through this entire day. And then she goes to work*! *I need to get it together and learn more from my wife's courage.* With that short emotional burst, he felt an enormous sense of relief.

Roberta did not get home until two hours later. Maci had woken from her nap and was so happy to see that the dogs and her daddy were still there. She squealed when she saw him enter the room and held out her arms saying, "Peese, peese, peese!" Once again Harvey felt a joy he had never known. It was not until Maci arrived that he even knew he could love a little person so much.

Maci was playing on the floor with her new toys as Harvey got up from the couch to fetch Roberta a glass of wine. There was leftover beef stew warming in the kitchen so that Roberta would not need to think about dinner. As soon as Roberta entered the room, Maci jumped up and ran to her mama. *What a satisfying feeling*, thought Roberta, *especially when you're being greeted by your own child.*

Her thoughts were interrupted as Harvey asked, "Why in the world did you need to go to the office while you're on leave?" He handed her the glass of wine as she removed her shoes and put her feet on the coffee table.

She said, "It was an emergency placement for a kid that's been in the system six years. It was a very important placement, too, something I need to talk with you about before it's finalized. The office called me while we were sitting at the park waiting after all the hoopla!" she said proudly.

"Since when do you need my permission to do your job, my dear beautiful wife?" he asked, kissing her on the neck.

"Since I found out Maci's brother had been put back into the system due to a failure in his foster care. The foster dad died of a heart attack and the mom needs to go to work to support her three other children."

"What? Maci's brother? Are you kidding me?" Harvey's voice cracked with emotion and excitement as he sat up straight on the couch."

"I got the call yesterday and asked them to bring me the file," she explained. "I wanted to review it first to see what had been going on with the child. The fact that it's Maci's half-brother piqued my interest. Imagine her having her own, real brother to watch over her."

She scanned his face to try to read his thoughts then continued. "He hasn't been abused like Maci was, but he does have strong abandonment issues. In the beginning his mother kept promising him she was coming back, but of course never did. When she failed to show, he was moved to another foster home and then moved again when the foster dad was transferred out of state. The boy's mother was contacted and wouldn't allow the courts to let him move with the family. He was moved one other time when the next set of foster parents lied on their application. It was that move that about did him in. He's been with this family for a while and the foster mom reports he has a lot of trust issues but he tries."

Harvey cleared his throat to speak, but she interrupted before he could make his case. "I know it's bad timing on our part since we just got Maci, but this is her brother. This could be a cure for them both. They may not understand the impact of being together, but I think it will be good for both. What do you think?" She asked in a shy, pleading voice.

Harvey sat for a few moments thinking, and then stood up. Roberta stared at him wondering what was going through his head. She had thought he would be elated with the idea but now she was unsure.

He took her hands in his. "May I speak now?" he asked. "Roberta, here's what I think, and I mean this with every fiber in my body." Harvey said looking straight into her eyes. She felt her heart sink. "I think if there are more siblings in the wings, we'll take them too!"

Roberta jumped to her feet and threw her arms around him.

"Just one thing, Roberta," Harvey interrupted the celebration. "If things get tough as we know they will, remember the quote, *'Blessed are the ones who takes care of widows and orphans.'* 'I am quite sure God said that. He gave me you and Maci. I'll gladly take whatever He wants us to do. I love you, Roberta. Despite all the fear and the worries that we've suffered, despite losing so many homes and a car, despite all of that, it was the best night of my life when I met you! With all this behind us now, we should no longer have to worry every day. We can go into our home knowing this is over."

He looked at her with deep and sincere love. "Now you can go out and change the world for these children, one child at a time, and I'll be right there with you, banging the doors down to help change laws, keeping the focus on these children in peril that live through broken promises every day. We'll do all we can to improve these children's lives and return them to the values that Trust can bring them. Only then will they understand the true meaning of the word."

ABOUT THE AUTHOR

Kenney Oldham Hayes is an author, speaker, musician, and retired banking executive with an industrious vision to illuminate compassion for abandoned children. She has been a CASA for 13 years and has served on boards awarding scholarships for young women.